"What were you thinking going over those falls?"

She should have expected the third degree from Ryan. Tori kept her voice low and replied, "That's not exactly what happened."

"So you weren't kayaking alone? You didn't go over the falls?"

Tori locked eyes with him. "I went to the river to travel in Sarah's path the day she died." She held back the furious tears that surged unexpectedly. "So I went kayaking."

"Why do you torture yourself?" His expression twisted into one of severe pain. "Is that why you went over the falls?"

Her heart might just rip open. He knew her better than that. "How could you even think that? I planned to turn back. But someone shot at me and hit the kayak. I tried to get away, and in the end, I had nowhere else to go. The falls grabbed me. I thought I was going to die."

Ryan's mouth hung open as if he couldn't quite absorb the full meaning of her words, and he appeared to search for an adequate response but came up empty.

"Someone tried to kill me."

Elizabeth Goddard is the award-winning author of more than thirty novels and novellas. A 2011 Carol Award winner, she was a double finalist in the 2016 Daphne du Maurier Award for Excellence in Mystery/Suspense, and a 2016 Carol Award finalist. Elizabeth graduated with a computer science degree and worked in high-level software sales before retiring to write full-time.

Books by Elizabeth Goddard

Love Inspired Suspense

Mount Shasta Secrets

Deadly Evidence

Coldwater Bay Intrigue

Thread of Revenge
Stormy Haven
Distress Signal
Running Target

Texas Ranger Holidays

Texas Christmas Defender

Wilderness, Inc.

Targeted for Murder
Undercover Protector
False Security
Wilderness Reunion

Visit the Author Profile page at Harlequin.com for more titles.

DEADLY EVIDENCE

ELIZABETH GODDARD

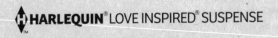

HARLEQUIN® LOVE INSPIRED® SUSPENSE

Recycling programs
for this product may
not exist in your area.

LOVE INSPIRED BOOKS

ISBN-13: 978-1-335-67919-2

Deadly Evidence

www.Harlequin.com

Printed in U.S.A.

Thy word is a lamp unto my feet,
and a light unto my path.
                    —*Psalms* 119:105

To the One who lights my path

Acknowledgments

Many thanks to my family, who put up with the many hours I spend on my computer crafting stories. Also a big thanks to my writing buddies, who encourage me along the way and patiently listen to my wild ideas and offer suggestions. My sincerest gratitude to my editor at Love Inspired Suspense, who gave me the opportunity to indulge my imagination, and to my agent, Steve Laube, who never stops working on behalf of his clients.

ONE

Wind River, Northern California

Victoria "Tori" Peterson glanced over her right shoulder as she rowed in her kayak, enjoying the view of the Wind River as it traversed through the shadow of Mount Shasta in beautiful northern California. Sweat rose on her back and beaded at her temples. Her muscles burned with each row of the double-bladed oar, but she welcomed the pain as the kayak glided on the river.

The exercise invigorated her. Got her heart pumping and the oxygen flowing.

It reminded her that she was alive.

Still, the uncanny sensation that someone was following her clung to her.

Another glance told her that no one was behind her. No one was on the river as far as she could see in the middle of a Monday afternoon.

The weekend was over and summer was ending—students were back in school.

She was utterly alone out here. Just how she wanted it.

This stretch of river was calm and slow and perfect for relaxing, contemplating and easing her troubled mind after the tragedy that had brought her all the way from Columbia, South Carolina. And for which she'd taken bereavement leave from her job as a special agent with the FBI.

She shrugged off the heaviness and focused on the sound of the oar cutting through the gentle flow as the current carried her forward. She needed this moment of solitude to get her through the next few weeks. Before the river became agitated and the current too strong—before Graveyard Falls—she would urge the kayak upstream against the current and back to where she had parked her car.

Sarah's car, actually. The thought of her sister brought on a surge of tears.

Focusing on the environment instead, Tori held them back and guided her bright blue kayak forward. The river twisted through the designated wilderness area and opened up into forests at the base of the mighty mountain—an inactive volcano. Mount Shasta could be seen from nearby Rainey, where she'd grown up.

The serene setting belied the violence that had taken place along the river only a few days before. Maybe it was the weight of that memory that punctuated the brisk mountain air and the combined scent of pine, hemlock, fish and fresh water with the feeling that someone had followed her.

Or maybe someone was really there.

She'd only taken leave last week in order to attend the funeral and hadn't so quickly forgotten to listen to her instincts. Still, she pushed the fears aside for the moment. Let the memories surface as she floated on the river that would eventually travel through Rainey on its way to empty into the Shasta River.

Growing up, she and Sarah had kayaked here all the time and camped in the area close to Mount Shasta—the mountain that had hovered over them their entire lives. Those memories made her laugh with joy even as she cried with grief. Those peaceful memories would forever be spoiled for Tori now.

But life went on around her. Nature blossomed and gloried in beauty as though nothing tragic had happened. The sun shone down on her. An eagle floated on the wind above her, its high-pitched whistle underscoring the wild environment around her.

And that eerie yet glorious sound nudged

her with the very question that had nagged her since her return. What had driven her to join the FBI, move across the country and leave behind the most beautiful place on earth? Leave behind her family, her sister and even a guy she could have married? Whatever those reasons, she couldn't quite remember them now. Instead, she would give anything to have stayed and gotten more time with her sister, Sarah.

She squeezed the oar and released her fury, taking it out on the river with each cut into the water.

The report of a rifle resounded, echoing through the woods and bouncing off the water.

Tori flinched and her gaze flicked to the woods behind her. She took in her surroundings again. Was someone simply out for target practice? She couldn't think of any hunting season open just yet, but she wasn't up-to-date on hunting season laws.

A thump shuddered through her kayak as another shot resounded. Her kayak had taken the hit. Someone was targeting her kayak.

Targeting her!

Her heart lurched as panic swelled. Pulse pounding, she pushed harder and faster with the oar.

She should have listened to her instincts. This was one of those moments when she hated to be right. Even if she hadn't wanted to believe it, someone had been following her. Somehow. Someway. They had waited here to ambush her. They'd planned their attack well. She couldn't possibly paddle fast enough or move out of the crosshairs if someone intended her harm.

Another bullet slammed into her kayak. Tori took hope in the miss. It seemed that whoever was shooting wasn't a trained sniper. Given the recent murders, she doubted they were just trying to scare her or warn her away. No, they were trying to hit her—and she couldn't count on them missing forever. Their next shot might hit the mark and injure her, or worse, kill her.

Her arms burned and lungs screamed as she sliced from the right to the left. Right, left, right, left, her body twisting with the movements, until it felt like she was one with the kayak.

God, please, please help me!

I can't die now! I have to find Sarah's killer!

Despite her efforts, she would never make it out of range if the shooter's rifle could handle the distance.

And if the shooter was determined.

Somehow she had to make this harder for the shooter. But how?

Ideas. She needed ideas. If she left the kayak and swam to the opposite shore, then what?

She'd be stuck over there at the shooter's mercy. She'd have to dash a hundred yards before she could hide in the tree line.

She couldn't count on being able to make it to safety that way. No. Tori needed to push farther on the river. Get much farther away and downriver and then she could possibly make her way to the trees before being gunned down. She'd be safe once she put enough distance between her and the shooter…except she had no idea how far the long-range weapon could shoot.

She had a feeling one of the shooter's shots would hit its mark if she stayed in his sights.

Another idea came to her. Tori gasped as she continued to push, putting more distance between her and the shooter. Hope built inside her that she would soon be out of range.

Would her idea work or would it kill her in another way? Before another bullet could slam into the kayak or into her body, she made a decision. Sucking in a big breath, Tori flipped the kayak as if to make a wet exit, only she remained in the kayak, floating on the river upside down, hoping instead to confuse the shooter. Make him wonder if she was planning to swim to shore, or if she'd drowned.

If he couldn't see her, she reduced his ability to kill her. Maybe.

He might still take a few shots, hoping to

kill her under the water. But she knew from her training that water distorted bullet trajectories, especially if the shooter wasn't experienced enough to compensate.

Holding her breath, she urged the kayak forward and out of range. Eyes open, she worked to avoid the outcropping of rocks thrusting toward her, but she wasn't quick enough. Pain lanced through her as the jagged edge of a broken rock gouged her shoulder. Her need to cry out almost cost her the last of her breath.

Lungs burning and screaming for oxygen, she held on to the last of her air a little longer, refusing to draw river water into her lungs. Had the shooter stopped, convinced he'd successfully shot her? Could he confirm that through his scope while she was beneath the water?

Her lungs spasmed. She was running out of time. The current grew stronger, the water more agitated. The kayak was getting closer to the falls.

Two options remained. She could exit the kayak and swim for it—or she could remain in the kayak and try to make the riverbank. She'd be on the opposite side from where she believed the shooter had perched to take his shots, and she'd be farther downstream by several hundred yards, but if the shooter had a good long-range rifle, he could still pick her off.

Using her hips and oar, she rolled the kayak back so she was above the water and sucked in a long breath. Her pulse raced.

Graveyard Falls roared in her ears and fear constricted her chest.

Too close. She was much too close to the falls. Had sending her over the falls been the shooter's intention all along?

Idiot. She'd been such an idiot!

She paddled backward, but the strong current had seized the kayak in its grip and wouldn't let go. The current was much too powerful for her—especially since she hadn't practiced this water sport in a long time. Tori groaned with the effort as she fought the current, the violent rapids and rush of water that would soon take her over. She fought to steer clear of the out-croppings of boulders that caused the water to boil even more. The river ensnared her, leaving her gasping and choking as she fought to survive.

Had another report sounded? She couldn't tell. Her chest swelled with fear. Good thing she hadn't exited the kayak—at least it could offer a measure of protection against the buildup of boulders and rocks near the falls. She desperately hammered the water in an effort to free the kayak but it was no use. The river pushed her forward toward the deadly waterfall. Despite her best efforts, she was going over the falls.

This wasn't called Graveyard Falls for nothing. Her breaths came fast, unable to keep up with the oxygen demand of her rapidly beating heart. Would these be her last breaths?

Graveyard Falls propelled the kayak, along with Tori, over the rapids, tossing her like she was a rag doll in a toy boat.

"Oh, no, no, no, no, no!"

Tori clung to her kayak as the waterfall took her over.

In those moments, every regret, every mistake she'd made, clung to her heart.

Ryan...

Detective Ryan Bradley's footfalls echoed down the sterile white hallway of Rainey General Hospital. Ten minutes ago, while in the middle of questioning someone in an ongoing investigation, he'd been informed that Tori Peterson was here and had asked for him.

She'd been injured, pulled from the river after going over Graveyard Falls. That news shocked him, to say the least. He was still stunned. Beyond concerned. He'd finished his interrogation, but unfortunately, he doubted he'd remember much of what was said. That was what he had a recorder for. At this moment, nothing mattered to him but Tori.

As soon as he'd heard that Tori had gone over those falls and survived, he'd wanted to rush to her side as if the last four years—and the all-important FBI job that she'd chosen over him—hadn't come between them. Ryan wanted to see for himself that she was all right. He wanted to hold her in his arms and feel her warm body against him and know deep in his soul that she was truly okay.

That was how he found himself rushing down the hallway toward her room—*whoa there, boy*—when what he really needed to do was slow his steps way down. That would give him time to decelerate his too-rapidly-beating heart and *get a grip*! Ryan had to find a way to redirect his mind away from his spiraling emotions that threatened to overtake him.

And most of all, he needed to focus on the facts. He didn't even know why she wanted to speak with him. Had she asked for him as a detective, or was this much more personal? Ryan should hope for the former, but his heart wished for the latter.

Traitorous heart.

He knew Tori was in town because of her sister's murder. Tori had attended the funeral last week, and she had obviously remained in town, perhaps to help her parents go through Sarah's things, or maybe just to comfort her parents.

Those were probably the excuses she told her family. But honestly, he could guess the real reason why she remained. He ground his molars and fisted his hands as aggravation churned in his gut. He'd figured it was just a matter of time before she sought him out—after all, he was the major crimes detective investigating the multiple homicides that had occurred two weeks ago and that had unfortunately involved her sister. He still couldn't believe it himself.

Tori's sister. Sweet Sarah Peterson. Gone forever.

Still, it was strange that Tori had asked for him after being pulled from the river. He was grateful she'd survived the falls, but he wanted answers about what was going on.

Spotting a vending machine—his salvation—Ryan stopped to grab coffee. He should join Procrastinators Anonymous, or was it United? After inserting and reinserting the cash into the slot until it finally pleased the machine, he pressed the appropriate buttons.

Coffee. *Give me coffee, black and strong*, he mentally demanded as the vending machine took its sweet time, for which he should be grateful. He needed a few more minutes to compose himself and appear like the disinterested, detached and impartial detective he strove to be.

His efforts were failing because he was definitely anything but detached and impartial. He couldn't believe how the mere thought of seeing Tori again affected him, especially knowing that she'd come so close to death. What was the matter with him? He let his thoughts sift through the last couple of weeks and focus on Tori and her family—their needs. Not his personal issues that had no bearing in the present.

Tori had lost her sister. She had to be a wreck. Ryan had been the one to give her parents the news, and it had been all he could do to keep his composure. Those were the moments when he hated this job.

A warm cup of coffee finally in hand, he downed the contents, then steeled himself. Enough procrastinating. He walked the rest of the way to room 225 and pressed his fingers against the partially open door. Voices drifted out. Tori's mother sounded upset. He leaned against the wall, deciding he'd give them a few moments. He popped in a piece of gum and skimmed his emails on his cell, except his mind was far from his cell phone.

Tori Peterson.

Once upon a time in the past, he'd thought he and Tori were on the same path. The same life track. He'd let his heart hope for something long-term between them. Then, when a door opened offering her the job of her dreams, she'd chosen that over him. Good for her. Bad for him. At the time, he'd been furious and hurt, and they hadn't parted on good terms.

Four years had changed his perspective. Now, he didn't blame her or hold anything against her. Instead, he saw it as a cautionary lesson not to set his heart on anyone. Time could heal all wounds, the saying went, and with time and experience, he'd learned his limits.

Ryan couldn't take that kind of heartache ever again.

The voices in the room died down and the room went quiet. Time for him to make his presence known. He knocked lightly on the door as he said, "Detective Bradley. Is it all right for me to come in?"

The door swung open to reveal Sheryl Peterson. She blinked up at him, relief in her face. "Come in, Ryan. I mean… Detective."

She eyed him as if to ask if it was okay that she called him by his first name. He smiled and gave a slight nod as he entered the room. He had known the Petersons for years—there was no need for formality with them.

Sheryl caught his arm, preventing him from going farther. She leaned in and spoke in a low tone. "I'm so glad you're here. She's not ready to listen. The doctor wanted to keep her another day. But she's planning to leave anyway. Can you talk some sense into her?"

Tori stepped out of the bathroom fully dressed. Next to the bed, she swayed a bit. Ryan rushed forward and caught her. He assisted her to the bed, where she should have stayed.

"I heard you lost a lot of blood during your fight with a waterfall," he said, his voice coming out gentle and caring. Not exactly what he'd been going for. He'd wanted to make it clear to her—to *both* of them—that he'd finally left their relationship in the past.

She lifted her gaze as if just now realizing he was there, that he'd been the one to assist her to the hospital bed. "Ryan. What…what are you doing here?"

Really? He'd been told that she'd asked for him. Maybe someone had made a mistake.

"I need to run an errand." Sheryl pursed her lips, still upset with her daughter. "I'll be right back. Ryan, please keep her in this room until I get back, okay?"

He nodded, but he couldn't promise anything. Sheryl disappeared and left Ryan and Tori alone in the room. It shouldn't feel awkward but it did.

"What were you thinking, taking that waterfall?" he asked. "Kayaking alone and going over the falls?"

Was she so devastated from the news of her sister's death that she had a death wish of her own? No. The Tori he'd known before would never take her own life—no matter what.

He fisted his hands, controlling the fury over her choices and fear for her safety that he had no right to feel. Swallowed the lump in his throat at the thought of what could have happened.

He was over her. Had been for a long time. But apparently the emotional equivalent of muscle memory hadn't gone away. When she was putting herself in danger, it was his instinct to worry.

Dumb instincts.

And he was done playing games or wasting time. "Why did you ask to see me, Tori?"

But he had a feeling he knew exactly why. Tori was here to find the person behind four murders, behind Sarah's murder, and as lead detective on this investigation, Ryan was about to get swept up in Tori's fast-moving current.

TWO

Ryan Bradley. Detective Ryan Bradley is in my room...

Blood rushed to her head.

Sitting on the edge of the hospital bed, Tori squeezed her eyes shut and breathed steadily. She had to regain her composure and stop her head from spinning. Enduring the guy's pensive gaze hadn't been in her plans for the day. She'd asked to see him? She didn't remember that part.

Tori focused on what had happened, mentally replaying images from her fight to survive the crushing falls. The helplessness as she tumbled through the air while water enveloped her. That suffocating, painful, drowning feeling of trying to catch enough air to live while unable to stop the force that could dash her against the rocks. All of it thrashed around in her thoughts even now.

Goose bumps rose on her arms.

Then she remembered… One of her last thoughts had been about Ryan. Her whole life—her decisions, mistakes and regrets—had flashed in her heart, and some of those biggest regrets revolved around him. No way could she tell him any of that here and now, if ever. She was embarrassed that she'd asked for him…but now that she thought of it, it was good that he was here. They *did* need to talk—not about her feelings, but about facts. But not here. "Can we go somewhere and talk?"

He studied her, obviously trying to decide if she was coherent or was suffering, both physically and emotionally, too much to think clearly.

He crossed his arms. A sentinel complying with her mother's demands to keep her here? "I don't think they want you to leave yet," he said.

Ah. He'd made his decision—the wrong one—and had sided with her mother. Tori didn't want to waste time at the hospital. She needed to find out who had killed her sister and why.

Then he shifted his posture, shoving his hands in his pockets. The way his jacket bunched up, she could see his department-issue weapon at his belt. "We can talk here," he said. "I'm assuming you want to talk about your sister's murder."

Amazing blue-green eyes stared down at her. His dark blond hair was slicked back and made him look far more serious than she remembered. He sported a Vandyke beard now, as was the style. In spite of herself, warmth flitted over her as she looked at him. How had he gotten more attractive since she'd seen him last?

Though maybe what really attracted her was that Ryan had that look of someone who knew what they were doing. The experiences of life shone on his face along with an intensity he hadn't had before. Not really a hardening, but more the look of someone focused and determined, who knew what he wanted and how to get it.

Just being in the room with him was almost too much.

A shiver ran through her.

She steadied her nerves and pushed to stand. "Yes. What I have to say has to do with Sarah, though not in the way you might think. But first you should know that I'm leaving. I've asked for discharge papers. I'm waiting on those now. Mom was wrong about them keeping me— she's the one who thinks I need more time here, not the doctor. So I'm leaving and I don't want to talk about my sister here."

His frown wasn't unexpected. He had to

know she wasn't satisfied with his investigation into the four murders, including Sarah's.

A social worker entered. "Ms. Peterson, I have your discharge papers and instructions. If you'll just sign and initial here." She laid out the yellow papers for Tori's signature and went over the instructions for the care of her wound.

After the social worker left, Tori smiled up at Ryan. "See?" Her mother would be furious when she got back here to find Tori had gone, but at least this way, she couldn't try to stop Tori from leaving. "But now I have a problem. I don't have a way out of here."

She thought to offer Ryan an innocent grin and blink as if to give him a hint—something she'd done in the past with him—but she had to steer away from giving him the wrong impression. No need to remind him of their past. Still, why wasn't he offering her that needed ride?

Instead, Ryan watched her. She never liked being analyzed. She supposed that was hypocritical since she did that a lot to others in her role as an agent. But being on the other end of that wasn't pleasant.

Finally he said, "I'll give you a ride. We can talk on the way. Where would you like to go?"

"Thanks. I'll text Mom and let her know that I'm with you and I'm okay."

"Are you really okay?" His wary eyes

showed just how worried he was. His concern went deeper than what he'd have felt for a fellow human being, or that of a detective who cared about people and bringing justice.

Ryan still cared about Tori.

Before panic could swell, she tore her gaze from him to text her mother. "I'll survive," she said.

At least, she hoped she would. And she would survive being in Ryan's presence, too. As for surviving the attempt on her life—would there be more attempts? Would one of them succeed? Her sister hadn't survived when someone had tried to kill her. Tori almost sagged under the weight of loss.

A tear trailed her cheek as she stared down at her cell. She wasn't sure what she was going to do without her sister in her life, but the truth was they hadn't exactly been in each other's lives that much since Tori had moved across the country. She'd told herself that they'd make up for lost time later, with phone calls or visits. That chance no longer existed now.

The knowledge that Sarah was gone, taken from this world by a murderer, flayed her and left her raw and bleeding.

She finished the text and looked up at him again. Waves of remorse and a thousand conversations she wanted to have with him rushed through her. Tori tried not to shudder. She didn't think he'd missed that, because Ryan had always been sharp and could read people even when they tried to hide something. *Especially* when they tried to hide something.

And years ago, he'd had an uncanny ability to read her. Had that changed?

Fifteen minutes later, they sat in a booth at a coffee shop. Tori had suggested they have their talk over coffee. Ryan had obliged. Coffee ordered, Tori resisted the need to take painkillers. Her shoulder had been wrapped, and she'd been given blood. She'd heal, with or without the painkillers, and she wanted her mind to stay clear. Somehow, she had to toughen up and see her way through this.

Ryan studied her. Scrutinizing her again?

"Would you please stop?" She rearranged the condiments.

Frowning, he shook his head. "Stop what?"

"Please stop looking at me like you're dissecting me. I'm not a frog. This isn't Biology 101."

"Sorry. I didn't mean to make you uncomfortable."

"No? I see you making mental notes that Tori Peterson doesn't like to be studied. I'm not a suspect, so you can quit with your intimidation tactics."

He shrugged. Then he shifted forward in the booth, a frank expression on his rugged face. "I'm worried about you."

"This is just a gash in my arm." He had no idea yet of the real reason why he should be worried. She vaguely remembered the pain of that rocky outcropping gouging her, but at least she wasn't dealing with a bullet wound to her head or her chest.

"What were you thinking, going over those falls?" He'd asked the question before and wanted an answer.

She kept her voice low and said, "It was not exactly my choice."

The waitress brought their coffee. Tori poured half-and-half in hers. Ryan sugared his up too much for her taste.

"What are you saying, Tori? That you weren't kayaking alone? That you didn't go over the falls?"

"See, this is what I wanted to talk about." She took a sip of coffee and let it warm her belly, then leaned back. She shut her eyes and calmed her breathing. Let herself remember.

Tori opened her eyes. "I thought I was going to die when I went over the falls. I fought to survive and somehow…somehow I did survive. I woke up and coughed up water. Maybe the couple who pulled me from the river revived me. I don't know. But I do remember now that I said your name, Ryan."

Deep lines carved into his forehead and around his mouth. "Tori, I—"

"I went to the river today to travel in Sarah's path." That, and she'd needed to remember what it was like to be on the river at the base of Mount Shasta. She'd needed to remember Sarah. "I'm staying in her house. I'm on bereavement leave now." She held back the furious tears that surged unexpectedly. "So I went kayaking along the river. That's what the four of them were doing that day, wasn't it? They were camping and had their kayaks, so we know they had planned to go down the river."

"Why would you torture yourself like that?" His expression twisted into one of severe pain. "Is that why you went over the falls?"

Her heart felt like it might just rip open at the realization that he really seemed to believe it had been a suicide attempt. She'd thought he knew her better than that. "How could you even think that? I planned to turn back. But someone shot at me and hit the kayak. I tried to get away and in the end, I had nowhere else to go but into the water. I thought I could get to shore once I put some distance between me and the shooter, but the falls grabbed me and wouldn't let go. You know how strong the current is the closer you get to Graveyard Falls."

Ryan's mouth hung open as if he couldn't quite absorb the full meaning of her words, and he appeared to search for an adequate response but came up empty. Tori decided to fill the silence herself.

"Someone tried to kill me."

Stunned at her claim, Ryan somehow found the strength to close his mouth. Then to form words. "Are you sure?" Entirely lame and inadequate words. He knew as soon as they escaped his lips, but especially after the glare she gave him. She didn't like that he'd questioned her.

As an FBI agent, she thought herself superior to him. He knew that with certainty because that was why she'd wanted to join the feds to begin with. And suddenly he was thrown back in time. He'd never been good enough for Tori Peterson. Nor would he ever be good enough.

But he didn't care to be good enough for her now. Finally, he could let go.

Keep telling yourself that.

"Of course I'm sure. Why would you doubt me?" She narrowed her eyes and studied him. Must be her turn to analyze him.

He wasn't intimidated by her FBI-schooled expression. Instead, he was terrified that her words could be true. "I didn't say I doubted you. You've been through a lot. You've suffered a great loss. I'm concerned, that's all." He wanted to believe that her memories of what happened were false memories brought on by the trauma and her injury. Ryan didn't want to even entertain the possibility that someone had actually tried to kill Tori.

"You don't believe me? I can prove it to you, Ryan. Let's go find the kayak. You can look at the bullet holes yourself. We can gather evidence together."

"You're not part of my investigative team."

She pursed her lips. "But I *am* going to investigate, whether you want me to or not, so wouldn't it make more sense to work together? Especially if the attack on me is in any way tied to Sarah's murder. What do you think, Detective Bradley? That Sarah's death was a random act of violence—four kids killed by someone out on a shooting spree while camping? Or that maybe they stumbled upon something they shouldn't have seen? Or did someone kill four kids to cover up one murder? On any of those possibilities, do you think the murders are drug-related?"

Okay. Well, sure, that it was drug-related was his working theory for now. Wasn't it almost always drug-related no matter the crime? He said nothing, wondering what she'd say next—what she'd reveal. She'd called the victims kids, but they had been in their twenties. Still, Tori considered Sarah her kid sister growing up and that obviously hadn't changed. He understood because he had three siblings himself.

Katelyn was his twin sister, then there was his brother Reece, who was two years older, and Benjamin—Ben—who was three years younger. He couldn't imagine losing any of them.

How was Tori even holding it together?

"Fine. You don't want to answer now. We can talk on the way to the river. Are we going or not?" Her determined tone and severe frown left no doubt as to her resolve.

Of all the times for him to crack a smile—but he couldn't control himself. He'd always loved it when she got fired up over something she believed in. So feisty and determined. Did she realize how much Sarah had idolized her? Sarah had wanted to be just like her sister, and had found her own passionate way to serve people by involving herself in social justice issues. Tori had taken a different route but fought for justice all the same. And when she was on the hunt for answers, nothing and no one could make her stop. He knew she was right that he wouldn't be able to stop her from investigating, but he'd torture her a few moments longer with a wry grin before he'd announce his decision.

Meanwhile, he took his time admiring her new look. She'd cut her long brown hair shorter so that it hung to her shoulders, and she'd dyed the silky tendrils a soft golden blond that was growing out and revealed hints of brown. Ryan remembered her smile—she'd always had the most amazing dimples that drove him wild and made him want to kiss her.

Even now, with the mere thought of it.

He cleared his throat and forced his impartial face in place. He was such a liar. "Let's go."

In his unmarked utility vehicle belonging to the Maynor County Sheriff's Department, he drove toward the river. He would radio for assistance once he got a look at the kayak himself to confirm Tori's claims. He wanted to see the bullet holes first. Ryan held on to the small hope that her memory of today's earlier events was off. If Tori really was being targeted for some reason, that would terrify him but also change the investigation.

As if sensing his need to contemplate what she'd told him, she kept quiet and left him to his own thoughts. He gripped the steering wheel too tightly as he steered the SUV through the small town of Rainey, the town where he'd chosen to live. Rainey had proven to be peaceful and quiet—a place he could go home to at the end of a long day of facing crime puzzles and criminals and simply relax and breathe in the fresh air.

But the murders two weeks ago—just outside of Rainey—had rocked his world. In fact, the whole town of Rainey had been shaken.

Ryan kept driving until he was on the long, curvy road that followed the Wind River. Tall trees hedged the road to either side on this part of the drive and he could barely make out the peak of Mount Shasta as he headed toward the camping and river rafting/kayaking area where Tori told him she had parked her vehicle.

Not far from where four people had been murdered.

He knew the spot well. Had been there too many times to count—with her, no less. He made to turn into the parking area but she touched his arm.

"You need to go all the way down to the base of the falls," she said. "My kayak is probably downriver, unless someone already picked it up."

She dropped her hand, but he still felt the spot where she'd touched him.

Of course the kayak would be downriver of the actual falls. He should have thought of that. Being this close to her, he couldn't think straight. But he'd give himself a break—he hadn't seen Tori in so long and now she'd been injured and could have died on those falls. He was allowed to be a little distracted under those circumstances.

"Maybe whoever shot at you already grabbed the kayak." And with the words, he realized he'd lost all hope that she'd been mistaken. He believed that someone had, in fact, shot at Tori Peterson.

Tori was a good agent, and despite the trauma and the grief of loss, she would know exactly what had happened. She'd been trained to have an excellent memory. She glanced his way with an arched brow as though she thought his words were simply more sarcasm.

"What? I believe you."

Her brows furrowed.

"No, really. I had hoped you were mistaken, I'll be honest."

His response seemed to satisfy her and her expression relaxed. "Let's hope we can find it."

"Agreed." He sighed. "We need to talk this through. I take it you think that whoever shot at you is somehow connected to Sarah's murder." And also Mason's, Connie's and Derrick's. Four people in their twenties just out camping and having fun, murdered.

"I think it's highly suspect, don't you?" She fumbled around in that big bag she called a purse.

Unfortunately, yes. He nodded and maneuvered the road. "I don't usually believe in coincidence. That's why I held on to the smallest of hopes that you were wrong about what happened."

He felt her glare again.

He glanced at her and then focused on the road. "A detective can hope, can't he? I didn't want to think that someone had tried to kill you, Tori. And the fact that they did brings up another question." How did he word this?

"Well, what is it?"

Might as well try. "Someone killed four people, leaving us to speculate on the reasons and focus a lot of resources on finding answers. Why would they draw more attention by shooting at you? What could they hope to gain with that attempt on your life? It doesn't make sense." Though when did murder ever make sense?

"I don't know. I think... I was close to the falls. Honestly, I think they had hoped to send me over to die and make it look like an accident. Maybe they had planned to make sure I was dead, but the couple found me first."

"But again—why?"

"Maybe they don't like Sarah's FBI sister digging into things and planned to head me off before I found out the truth."

Ryan did not like to hear those words. They meant Tori's life was in ongoing danger. Man, did he wish this wasn't happening. Those kids were gone and that was tragic news. It was his job to find their killer, but how did he also prevent another murder, and Tori's at that? His insides twisted up in knots. Tori was an FBI agent and had faced dangerous situations in her job, but that didn't make him feel any better about her safety. On-the-job danger was one thing— someone actively trying to kill her was another.

Finally he came upon the sign for the trailhead and boat launch at the bottom of the falls. He parked at a gravel parking spot near the river, just down from where it spilled over Graveyard Falls. On weekends and during tourist season, the place would be crowded. People liked to hike along the narrow path between boulders, to get closer to the waterfall and watch the majesty of the beast, as well as feel the spray hitting their faces and getting them wet.

Tori reached for the door. He touched her arm and she held back from opening the door. "What is it?"

"Before we get out, there's more I want to

say." Before finding Tori's kayak with a bullet hole or two in it messed with his head. "My working theory has been that the murders are drug-related. Sarah's boyfriend, Mason Sheffield? Turns out he had some priors. Mostly the usual stuff with drugs. Maybe he was dealing or stole something. Sarah got involved with the wrong guy. It happens, Tori, you know it does."

She shifted in the seat to face him. "So they take out a group like that? And the law comes down on them?"

"I agree. That wasn't smart."

Tori shook her head vehemently. "I'm not buying your theory. Or rather, I'm not ready to settle for it."

Ryan held his temper in check. Did she realize she'd insulted him? But he was curious, too. "So let's have it. What do you think happened?"

"Killing several people in a group out camping could be a ploy to take the focus off just one murder."

"You brought that up earlier. That doesn't mean drugs aren't involved."

She stared straight ahead and heaved a sigh. "It's not like Sarah to date someone who was into drugs."

"I hear you. I didn't want to believe it, either, but in the world we live in, our loved ones are getting involved in dangerous things left and right. And family ignores it, chooses not to believe it, or somehow they live in complete ignorance." He drummed the console between them. They needed to get out and find the kayak. This wasn't getting them anywhere.

"If it was all stuff from years ago then I can see Sarah giving him a second chance," Tori said. "Maybe he wanted to change. Maybe she was helping him to get clean."

"I can see that, too."

When Tori said nothing more, he finished what he'd started. "Bottom line is that, regardless of the reasons, the murders are heinous crimes that make no sense. But even if we manage to find answers, making sense out of the murders won't bring Sarah back. It won't change anything."

"Is this your way of suggesting I stay out of it?"

He shrugged. "You have a job and a life back in South Carolina, Tori. It's my job to solve this. Staying here won't bring her back." He braced himself for her reaction and when it didn't come like he expected, he released the breath he'd held. The truth was that he understood why she felt she had to stick around and try to find Sarah's killer. If he were for some reason assigned to another case and removed from this one, he would still work to solve Sarah's murder. He wanted to make sense out of her death, too.

"Look—" she released a sigh "—murder can never be resolved, not really. Finding out who did this and why will be enough for me. But nothing we've said here explains why someone shot at me."

She was right. Taking her out, too, made no sense. But if that was what had happened, then he doubted the danger was over. He knew she wouldn't leave until the murderer was caught, which meant he would have to figure out how to protect a capable special agent who didn't think she needed protection. And the worst part?

Ryan feared he would fail.

THREE

Making their way to the falls, they trekked alongside the fast-moving river, Tori leading Ryan, who trailed a few paces back. The roar grew louder with their approach. The force of the falls up ahead compelled the river forward, causing it to be swift and dangerous. The memories of the moment Graveyard Falls pulled her down and over lashed at her insides.

She hesitated for a moment, unsure if she could keep up the search for her kayak, and stopped to watch the river. While swirling in that vortex, she'd feared she would die.

Had Sarah known she was going to die? What were her last thoughts? Tori hated to think of the terror her sister must have endured. Had Sarah also spoken someone's name in those moments before her death? And if she had, whose name would she have said?

A loved one's?

Or the killer's?

A shudder crawled over her.

"You okay?" She was freed from her musings by the arrival of Ryan's sturdy form next to her.

"Sure."

Tori shook off the morbid thoughts and started hiking again. She turned her focus instead to this path next to the river and the unbidden memories floating to the surface. She and Ryan had hiked this trail on multiple occasions when they were seeing each other. Probably like the young couple who had pulled her from the river earlier in the day.

Back then, it had been just the two of them. Hand in hand. Falling deeper in love with each passing day.

And they'd shared more than one amazing kiss right here when no one else was around. Her chest grew tight.

Was he thinking about those kisses, too? She hoped not, but when she glanced over her shoulder and caught his pensive gaze, she knew where his mind had gone—to them as a couple before she left.

Pain cut through her at how different things were now. Instead of a couple in love enjoying a nature walk, they were now joined together only by the need to find a killer before he struck again. Was that why she'd said his name earlier? Because he was the investigator on Sarah's case? Tori had thought she was going to die, and maybe she'd wanted to somehow let Ryan know that her death hadn't been an accident. She'd thought of him—her last coherent thought before the greatest struggle of her life, and then, she'd huffed out his name when she came to.

If she hadn't said his name, they would probably be here together now anyway, since she would have gone to him to report the attack on her as soon as she left the hospital. That she'd said his name shouldn't matter so much, but it bothered her and she wanted to know why. She would have to think about that later, though. Much more pressing matters needed her attention.

She hiked forward, closing in on the falls.

The flash of color on the other side of a rocky outcropping drew her attention. "There. I see a kayak."

"Fortunately it's not across the river," he said. "Are you sure it's yours?"

"It looks like mine, and if it's not, then that could mean someone else went over the falls." She didn't think that was the case.

Spotting the kayak exhilarated her. Now they were getting somewhere. Not that she feared he doubted her words—not anymore, at least—

but the kayak with a bullet hole or two in it would go a long way to boost her theory, one she hoped Detective Bradley was also formulating.

They made their way around boulders and roots, and then to the edge of the riverbank where the broken kayak had wedged between rocks. Tori gasped at the sight. She wrapped her arms around herself.

That could have been her body. Broken and lifeless.

Ryan's frown deepened. He appeared shaken as he pressed his hand over his mouth then rubbed his chin.

Then, seeming to pull himself together, he reached in the pocket of his jacket and tugged out a small camera. "Don't worry. We'll get Jerry, our tech, out here now that we know it's part of a crime scene, but I want to take my own pictures just in case."

Ryan walked around the kayak and took photographs from various angles.

She peered at the front portion. "See, just there. A bullet hole."

"Here's another." He pointed, then crouched and took close-ups of the holes.

Tori looked around for the oar, but she doubted she'd find it. "I'm surprised a bullet went through the material, but I guess it all depends on the caliber of bullet and the quality of the kayak materials."

"Right."

"We'll have to go up above the falls to look for rifle shells," she said. "It's a big area to search."

"Finding a shell doesn't mean it belonged to this particular shooter," he said. "We need bullets, too."

"Your lab can get ballistics, can't they?" Tori had to be careful what she said. Ryan was probably kind of touchy about the limited resources of his job compared to hers, and she didn't want to sound superior. But, well, the FBI had superior training, facilities and labs. The best, in fact.

He pursed his lips and eyed her as he got on his radio and asked for evidence collection and retrieval of the kayak. "We'll need to wait here to make sure no one disturbs it intentionally or otherwise, although if they had intended to do that, I think the kayak would already be gone."

Tori started toward the falls. "I'll hike up topside and look for rifle shells. There were more than two shots fired, even though there are only two bullet holes in my kayak."

Ryan grabbed her arm and gently squeezed as he pulled her toward him. "Are you serious?

What makes you think whoever shot at you won't try again? You're not going up there."

"In that case, what am I even doing out here with you?"

"Good question." He worked his jaw as if angry with her. Angry with himself.

His concern for her chipped away at the wall around her heart. She reminded herself that his reaction didn't mean that he cared for her on a personal level. Of course he would be this concerned for anyone. Right?

"I don't think the shooter is still here," she said. "When I got on the river, I had an eerie feeling. You know the one. I felt like someone was following me. Like someone was watching me. But I don't sense that now."

He scraped a hand through his hair, messing with the slicked-back look. "Come on, you can't trust a feeling like that. Not saying you should ignore it when you sense that someone is watching you, but you can't be certain you're safe just because it doesn't feel like anyone's watching you." He searched the ground near the kayak. For footprints? Too many hikers had been by the kayak today for forensics to find anything. After a minute, he lifted his gaze to look at the woods. A group of senior citizens hiked up the trail toward them, lost in their conversation. They smiled and bade them a good day as they passed.

The shooter wouldn't try again here today with people out on the trail, would he? The couple who'd found her hadn't been at the top of the falls where she'd been forced over. She'd been alone up there when he'd shot at her. Tori rubbed her arms and stared at the woods. She absolutely wouldn't let fear take hold of her or stop her. "We have to find who did this, Ryan."

Her comment drew a severe look from him, one that she knew well. Tori averted her gaze.

"Don't you have a job back in South Carolina to get back to? How long are you staying again?" The friction between them edged his tone. "Bereavement leave doesn't give you but a week or two, does it?"

"I… I don't know," she said.

"What?"

She hung her head. Closed her eyes. "You're right. Officially, I only have two weeks, but I'm considering taking an indefinite leave."

"Why would you do that?"

A feral emotion flashed in his gaze. She understood the deeper meaning behind his questions. She'd given him up. She'd left him for an FBI career—now he wanted an answer as to why she would give it all up for this investigation when she wouldn't give it up for him. She offered a one-shoulder shrug. "Mom and Dad are devastated. They've lost a daughter, Ryan." She looked in his eyes and took in the blue-green hues. "I need to be here for them and…"

Something shifted behind his gaze—and for the life of her, she couldn't tell if it was good or bad. Again, she had the strong sense that he still cared about her. That he'd never stopped. Her next words would drive an even bigger wedge between them. She'd hurt him terribly when she'd chosen her career with the FBI over a relationship with Ryan. She'd wanted more than working law enforcement in a northern California county. She could have taken a job and worked with him, but she'd taken the FBI's offer.

Tori drew in a breath. She might as well say it. "I need to make sure her killer is caught."

He lifted his chin to search for words in the bluest of skies. "And you don't trust me to do that."

"That's not what I said."

"But it's what you meant. You can't go home because you don't think we'll find the killer without your help."

"Ryan, please tell me that you understand. You would do the same if it was one of your siblings, someone you loved dearly, no matter who was investigating."

When he looked at her again, she saw resignation. "You're not here in your capacity as an FBI agent, so I'm going to ask you not to interfere. Trust me to do my job, Ms. Peterson."

The air rushed from her lungs. *Oh, come on.* She took a step toward him, trying to think of what to say to get him to see, though she wasn't sure why she wanted him to understand. "Ryan, please. I… I trust you to do your job. I promise I won't interfere with your investigation."

He nodded and huffed, then surprisingly gave her a wry grin. "I hear what you're saying. And what you're *not* saying. I know you, Tori. You have your own investigation going."

Sarah… "While you're looking for the person who killed four people, I'm looking for the person who killed one person. Sarah. You can't get in her head like I can. You can't walk in her shoes or think the way she would have thought. That's all I'm doing." She and Sarah were sisters. No one could know her better, even with the fact that Tori had lived far from Sarah for four years.

His forehead furrowed. Eventually he would come to the same conclusion about whom the murderer had intended to kill—the one target—if he hadn't already.

In the distance, they saw two county SUVs pull up behind Ryan's unmarked vehicle.

"Looks like the wait is over." He sounded relieved. "I can't stop you from investigating on your own. But don't make me charge you with obstruction. If you find evidence, please call me."

Even a private investigator looking into a major crime like murder could get charged with obstruction if he or she wasn't careful. "I will, I promise." She eyed him. "I trust you with this case, honestly." More than he would ever know or believe. "And you're a good detective. You're a good man, Ryan."

He stared at her as if he didn't know how to take the compliment, but she saw the doubts swimming in his eyes. Being a county detective hadn't been good enough for her. Before emotions rushed through her, she looked at the river. She shouldn't think about the past, but she almost regretted the choices she'd made that caused her to lose him.

Almost.

Because truly regretting her choices would mean she'd made the wrong ones. And she couldn't accept that.

While Ryan spoke to his team of deputies and his techs who would process and then transport the kayak, Tori waited near the river. Was the shooter out there somewhere, watching?

Two techs began processing the kayak—taking pictures and documenting everything. Tori was glad Ryan hadn't just hauled it in his SUV as if it had no importance. The slightest detail could be vital in a case like this.

He left his team to work and approached her. "You ready to go?"

"I thought we were going to look up top for rifle shells. We could help those deputies search for evidence. We aren't doing anything."

"Let the county sheriff's department handle it. I'm taking you home."

Though she didn't need the lead investigator acting as a chauffeur, how else would she get home? Dad had already gotten her car from the river. Back in his SUV, Ryan steered them toward town.

"Is there any remote chance that the fact someone targeted you has to do with something unrelated to Sarah—maybe one of your past cases?"

"I suppose anything is possible, but it's not probable."

They remained quiet for the remaining miles back to town. As he drove down Main Street in Rainey, her mind constantly flashed to memories of them together. It seemed so strange to be with him again, only for an entirely different reason than because they simply wanted to be together.

A gut-wrenching reason. Her breath hitched and she squeezed the hand rest.

"I keep asking if you're all right." He steered into the driveway of Sarah's small bungalow and parked. "You keep telling me that you are. But you're not okay. I'm worried about you, Tori."

"You've said that." Tori hung her head. She didn't want to get into this conversation with him. Why did he have to keep asking? Why did he have to care? Of course she wasn't okay.

"Is it me?" he asked.

That question brought her head up to look at him. "What do you mean?"

"Is being here with me too much for you? Too awkward? I know we're both trying to stay focused on the case, but maybe it's too much. Maybe it's just too hard to work together."

And you want to avoid me, Ryan? She kept the question to herself. "Even if it's too hard, we have to push past that. We can't change it."

"We can. You can go back to work in South Carolina. Be safe. Let me find who killed these people. Your sister. I don't need your help."

Tori had no response to that. She got out of the vehicle, slammed the door and stomped up to the home that reminded her so much of

Sarah. She remembered when her sister had picked it out. Sarah had emailed so many pictures to Tori. She'd been so excited to find such a cute place to live in on her own.

Oh, Sarah...

What had happened to her was wrong on so many levels. Why couldn't Ryan understand that Tori could not leave this alone? She wanted to look Sarah's killer in the face. And deep in her heart, she wanted to be the one to bring him down.

At the door, she fumbled for the keys in her purse with shaking hands and then finally unlocked the door. Ryan remained in his vehicle, making a call, waiting for her to get safely inside. She wished he would hurry up and leave.

Inside, she slammed the door and pressed her back against it, her heart pounding for no other reason than she was upset with Ryan. Upset with herself. Upset that this nightmare was real. Tears leaked out the corners of her eyes.

She swiped them away. No time for grieving.

Tori needed an escape from the events of the last weeks, days and hours. Unfortunately, Sarah's home was full of reminders instead. She shoved herself away from the door and dropped her bag on the table in the foyer. Dad had retrieved it from the car and Mom had brought it up to the hospital. Mom. She'd better text—

Clank, clank...

Tori froze. She listened.

The hair on her arms rose. Someone was in the house just down the hallway.

She pulled her weapon from her bag. Even on leave, she was required to always carry her FBI-issued weapon with her.

Weapon at the ready, she crept down the hallway toward where the sound had come from and cleared the first room. That left only one more room. Heart pounding, she whipped the weapon around as she stepped through the open door. "Freeze!"

A masked man stood much too close—her mistake—and he knocked the SIG from her grasp. She fought him, but with her injured shoulder, she struggled. Still, Tori was determined to best him. Somehow, she needed to get to her gun on the floor. Tori punched him in the solar plexus for good measure, then slammed his throat.

He coughed and gasped, but pulled out his own weapon—a nine-millimeter Glock.

Oh, no...

Tori dove into the hallway as gunfire exploded.

At the crack of gunfire, Ryan's heart jackhammered.

He tossed his cell aside and radioed dispatch

that shots had been fired and to send backup. But with Tori in danger, he couldn't wait for them. He jumped from the SUV and pulled his Glock from his holster all in one smooth motion.

Please let me be wrong, please let me be wrong.

But it was hard to mistake the sound.

He sprinted up the driveway toward the front door. The distinct sound of glass shattering resounded from the back of the house.

Weapon held at low ready, he quickly crept along the side of the bungalow, cautious near the bushes in case someone hid behind them. At the back corner, he peeked around, prepared to face off with a possible perp.

But he saw no one in the neat backyard that included a blue-and-white-striped hammock. His heart kinked as he pictured Sarah relaxing in that hammock. But there was no time to think about what had been lost. Ryan kept his weapon ready to aim and fire and continued all the way into the backyard to make sure it was clear.

At the back of the house, he found the shattered glass and the window that had been broken.

"Tori!"

While he didn't want to destroy any evidence,

his primary focus was on finding her. He approached the window carefully and glanced inside. He saw nothing. "Tori?"

There was no response. His heart rate ratcheted up.

Lord, please let her be okay.

He ran around to the front of the house and, shoving the door open, forced his way inside. "Tori! Are you okay?"

"Here. I'm in here."

Following the voice, he rushed into the hallway and found her on the floor. His pulse thundered in his ears as he crouched next to her. "Tori, honey…"

Sweat beaded her face and blood soaked her arm. His heart pounded. "You're hurt! Someone shot you?"

"No, it's just my wound broke open."

He wanted to reach for her but was afraid to make her pain worse. "What happened?"

"First, help me get up."

He assisted her to her feet.

She bent over her thighs as if to catch her breath, then leaned against the wall, her hand pressed to her chest. "Someone was in the house. A masked man. I walked in on him. We fought, but my shoulder isn't so good, so he got the best of me."

Blood soaked her shoulder and arm now.

While she talked, he grabbed towels from the bathroom, then pressed one against her shoulder. "We need to stop the bleeding."

"I made a mistake and he was too close to me when I confronted him. He was able to knock my gun away. We fought and I almost had him, but then he pulled a gun of his own. That's when I dove into the hall. He broke the window and climbed through it to the backyard."

Tori pressed the towel against her shoulder, relieving Ryan of the task.

"He didn't pursue you into the hallway?" *Thank You, God.* He couldn't bear to think of how this could have ended—and on his watch, no less.

"No. I'm not sure why he didn't just flee out the front door, but maybe he was afraid he would run into you. I'm also not sure why he didn't try to…" She trembled.

Kill her? Was that what Tori would have said had she completed her sentence?

"I'm not sure why he didn't finish the job," she said.

His insides quaked. Ryan never ever wanted to see his Tori, tough FBI agent Tori Peterson, this shaken again.

His Tori?

"Oh, honey." He took her into his arms, careful of her shoulder.

She cried into her hands against his chest, the bloodied towel pressed between them against her shoulder. Tori had always been the strongest person he knew—but she'd been through so much. These latest attacks meant she'd barely had time to grieve over the loss of her sister. But he supposed that this *was* how she'd chosen to grieve—by fighting back and trying to find Sarah's killer. Tori's job was all about law and justice, and for her sister to be murdered chafed in every way.

Sirens rang out in the distance and grew louder.

Finally...

"I called reinforcements when I heard gunfire." His chin rested on the top of her head, stirring memories of him holding her in his arms—but those times from their past couldn't be more different than the current situation.

She sniffled and stepped away. Swiped at her eyes. "I'm sorry. I don't know what came over me."

Strong Tori was back again, and strong Tori refused to show any weakness. She left him standing there and stomped into the bedroom. The guest bedroom...he knew that because he was the detective on the case, and he'd already been through the house in search of clues. Ryan trailed her.

"This is my FBI-issued gun." She pointed at the weapon lying on the floor on the other side of the room. "He knocked that out of my hands. He was wearing gloves, but maybe there could still be DNA. Certainly not prints, though."

"Jerry will look it over first to make sure."

"Okay. I want it back as soon as possible." She moved to the window. "You already know that he broke the window getting out. While your people sweep this place for prints and evidence, I'll canvass the neighborhood."

Right. He fisted his hands on his hips. "You really can't let it go, can you?"

She scrunched her face but her gaze swept the room. "What are you talking about?"

"You are not the law around here anymore. You gave that up, remember? Your FBI credentials don't change the fact that this murder case isn't in your jurisdiction." Nor would she be allowed to work it professionally because Sarah was her sister.

"Fine. I'm going for a walk then. I need to get my head together."

Ryan grabbed her arm. "You're not going anywhere."

"Get your hands off me."

He released her slowly but stayed close. "Tori, just calm down. You're bleeding, remember?" He lifted the towel and held it out to her.

She scrunched her face and took the towel, pressing it against her shoulder again. She wasn't thinking clearly, either, or else she would suggest looking at the rest of the house. Maybe the intruder had been in Sarah's home searching for something. Was anything missing? But Ryan wouldn't bring that up just yet. Tori needed to see the doctor again, and she'd only insist on looking through the house if he brought that to her attention. Discovering if something was missing could wait. Her well-being came first.

Deputies finally entered the home. Tori appeared pale and remained shaken, so Ryan stayed near as he explained what had happened. Her official statement could be given later. Ryan escorted her out of the house. "I need to take you back to the hospital so you can get that looked at."

"I'm supposed to replace the bandage anyway." She shrugged. "I'm fine to take care of it myself."

He'd expected her resistance and knew the best method to counter it was to redirect the conversation. "I'm considering this more than a simple break-in."

"You mean…"

He nodded. "Yes. I told you I don't believe in coincidence. My working theory—which I'm hoping the evidence will confirm—is now that Sarah was the primary target, not Mason or any of the others. For now, I'm going to investigate as if the rest of them were in the wrong place at the wrong time or killed to throw off the investigation. Satisfied?"

She offered a tenuous smile. "Yes."

Outside, he ushered her back to his SUV. "I'll take you to the ER first."

"Ryan, I was serious when I said I would be fine. My shoulder just needs a new bandage. There's nothing more the doctor can do, really. It needs time to heal."

"So let it heal and stop fighting criminals. Do we have a deal?" He tossed her a wry grin, and was rewarded with a half smile.

"If you stop insisting on taking me to the hospital."

"Fine. Then is it all right if I take you to your parents' for the night?"

She nodded.

"Once we're finished processing the bungalow and release the crime scene, you can go back to staying there, but I wouldn't advise it. Whoever broke in can try again. Next time you might not be so fortunate." He hated saying those words. Hated that Sarah had somehow made an enemy, and Tori had put herself in the line of fire to find the person responsible.

Tori said nothing more, which troubled him. Normally she would have objected or put forth her opinion, but even the strongest FBI agent could become traumatized when they had lost a loved one *and* been personally targeted. A female officer would pack a small bag of clothes for Tori's stay with her parents and deliver it. He drove the SUV from the quiet neighborhood where Sarah had lived to the Petersons' home only a mile away. After parking in the driveway, he ushered Tori to the house.

Tori knocked softly and then opened the door, peeking her head in. "Mom? Dad? It's me."

She stepped through the door, and Ryan remained on the porch, unsure if he was invited. Tori glanced at him.

"Tori?" Sheryl appeared in the foyer. "I thought you were with—" Her eyes caught on Ryan. "Well, don't just leave him standing there. Come on in, Ryan."

He looked at Tori, searching her eyes for reasons he couldn't explain. He should get back to his investigation. He couldn't read her. Did she want him to stay or...

"Are you coming or what?" she asked.

He shrugged. "I can only stay a few minutes."

Sheryl gasped when she saw Tori's arm.

"See, I told you they let you out too soon! We need to take you—"

"Mom, please. I just need some fresh bandages." Tori headed down the hallway like she was a disgruntled teenager, Sheryl on her heels.

Arms crossed, Tori's father stepped from the kitchen area and watched them go. "What happened?"

Ryan was glad he'd stayed for a few minutes, after all. He wasn't entirely sure how much he was ready to share with her parents, but since it appeared that Tori truly was in danger, they needed to know what was going on for their safety and hers. He was glad for the opportunity to explain things to her father; then David could figure out the right way to tell Sheryl.

As Tori's father listened to Ryan detail the events of the day, his face paled. Ryan almost regretted telling him, but he needed all the help he could get to protect Tori.

Tori and her mother stayed in the bathroom redressing the wound and Ryan bade David goodbye. He had work to do. On their porch he took in the surroundings of the middle-class neighborhood and hoped Tori would be safe here.

But he knew that once she was able, Tori would stay at the bungalow again—tracing Sarah's steps, she'd said. Those steps could lead her right to her own death.

Ryan couldn't let anything happen to her. For her sake, for her parents' sake and for his own sake.

He was a homicide detective, but he'd give that up in a heartbeat to be her bodyguard. If she would let him.

He knew Tori would say she didn't need him.

She never needed him—not in the past, and not now.

But this time, that wouldn't stop him.

FOUR

The morning sun broke through the crack between the drapes, startling Tori awake and away from the grips of her nightmare. Heart pounding, she bolted upright and reached for her weapon—but it was gone.

Just calm down. She drew in a few long breaths. They'd taken her gun to look for fingerprints.

It took her a breath or two to remember that she was in her old bedroom in her parents' home—the home where she and Sarah had grown up. Mom hadn't changed much in the room. She'd taken down the posters of teenage idols and replaced them with Scripture-laced nature pictures. Tidied up the room a bit and, oh, replaced Tori's bed with a smaller twin bed. No wonder she hadn't slept all that well. She was accustomed to spreading out in the queen-size bed she'd purchased for her apartment back home.

Home.

And just where was home exactly? Was it here in California or was it back in South Carolina? She pushed aside the complicated musings—too much to think about at seven in the morning.

She eased back down in bed, surprised her mind had finally let her sleep. She tried to recall the nightmare, but nothing clear came to mind and she was grateful she couldn't remember. Still, the dream had left her unsettled. Her shoulder ached, and even itched a little. That was good. That meant it was healing.

The aroma of bacon and eggs pulled her all the way out of bed. She might as well get up to face the day. She slipped into comfy sweats and a T-shirt and meandered down the hallway with a yawn, then made her way to the kitchen, where she found Dad cooking breakfast.

He glanced up from frying bacon. "Hey, sleepyhead." No matter that she was in her thirties and was an FBI agent, he still talked to her like she was his little girl. Tori wasn't sure she would have it any other way.

"Morning." She wouldn't add the word "good." Nothing about it was good. She grabbed a mug from the cabinet and poured the rich dark coffee blend they all preferred. Tori breathed it in as she shoved onto a tall seat at the counter.

Dad smiled as he moved bacon from the pan to a plate, but despite the smile, a persistent, aching sadness poured from his gaze, and that, she understood completely. Her heart ached with the pain of loss they all shared.

She took a drink of coffee, hoping her thoughts would come together. "Dad, you don't have to cook me breakfast. Or even sound cheery for my sake. We're all still shaken over what happened. It's going to take us a long time to get over…" She couldn't even say her sister's name.

He plated the eggs to go with the bacon and set the dish on the counter in front of her. "You're still alive and with us, Tori. I intend to make the best of every moment with you. You need your energy, so eat up."

Tori obliged and crunched on a bacon strip. "Where's Mom?"

"She went to the store to grab orange juice."

Tori's favorite. Mom had done that for her. Oh, man. She sighed. This was going to be a long day. While on the one hand she appreciated what her parents were doing, she knew they would smother her if she let them. Hadn't the whole reason she'd come back to stay for a while been to comfort *them*? Still, maybe they could all comfort each other. Tori knew she often wasn't willing to admit when she needed emotional support. But maybe this time she should give in to it. Their encouragement could very well sustain her through trying to find Sarah's killer.

Tori heard the sound of the front door opening, then closing, and in rushed her mother with a few plastic sacks of groceries. She set them on the counter and smiled at Tori—that same pain was raw and unfiltered behind her gaze.

"That looks like more than orange juice," Tori said.

"Well, you know how it is. You go in for one thing and leave having spent a hundred dollars more than you intended." Mom poured juice into a glass and sat it in front of Tori. "Drink up."

Tori finished the eggs and bacon and drank the juice while her father ate his breakfast quietly and Mom cleaned up the mess he'd made. Tori carried both their plates over to the sink, rinsed them and then stuck them in the dishwasher. She turned to find her mother wiping down the counter.

Still no words. No one knew what to say.

"Thanks, Mom. Thank you both, but you don't have to do this."

Mom's eyes teared up as she shrugged. "What? What are we doing? We almost lost you, too."

Dad gave Tori a warning look, as if she'd said

something wrong. Truth was, anything she said would be the wrong thing.

Tori rushed around the counter and hugged her mom. "I'm sorry," she said.

Dad hugged them both. As warm and comforting as the embrace was, it was also steeped in sadness. She could drown in all this grief, and she had to somehow stay afloat.

Finally she backed away and wiped at her own eyes. "I can't... I can't find out what happened to Sarah like this. I need to focus."

Tori headed for her bedroom. A female deputy had brought a few of her belongings over to the house from Sarah's bungalow last night. Tori should shower and get dressed for the day.

"Wait, Tori, please." Mom rushed after her.

Tori hadn't meant to upset her mom. She turned to face her. "I'm here, Mom, for as long as you need."

"Please, come back to the living room and sit down. Your father and I want to talk to you."

Uh-oh. Tori followed Mom down the hallway to the comfortable living area and the sectional sofa. "I'd prefer to stand."

Dad made his way to the living room and joined them. Mom was the only one to sit.

Dad crossed his arms. "You mentioned that you were considering an indefinite leave or quitting your job so you could stay here. Now that we know your reason for staying would be to look for the killer, we want you to go home. Go back to your job. Please, Tori. We can't lose you, too, and if you stay here, you're in danger."

"What?" She hadn't realized she'd made her decision yet until this moment. "I can't go back, Dad. I can't go back to work on investigating other crimes when my mind will always be on finding Sarah's killer. Don't you want justice for her?"

"Ryan can give us that, Tori," Mom said. "You should trust him."

"I do trust him." She rubbed her arms. But apparently not as much as her parents did. What was the matter with her anyway?

Dad approached and hugged her again. He released her and gripped her shoulders to level his gaze at her. "Mom and I will come to stay out there in South Carolina with you. We'll do anything we need to do."

They were overreacting, but could she really blame them? They were terrified for her, and she hated doing this to them.

Mom tugged tissues from a box on a side table. "We considered moving even before yesterday. There are just too many memories here. I don't know if I can stand it. We could move to be close to you."

A lump grew in Tori's throat. "But you don't

have to move to be close to me. I'm here. And
you don't want the person who took Sarah from
us to scare us away. Sarah wouldn't want you
to leave one of the most beautiful and amazing
places in the world because you don't want to
be reminded of her." The words sounded more
cruel than she'd intended.

*But I moved away from the most beautiful
place... And people who loved me. A man who
loved me.*

Mom's eyes teared up again. "Please, just
consider it."

She nodded. "Okay. I promise I will." That
was the least she could do.

Tori turned and hurried back to the bedroom.
She fell onto the bed.

"God, what am I going to do?" *They're going
to drive me up the wall.*

When all was quiet in the house, she snuck
out of her room to snag another cup of coffee.
Dad had made another pot and left her mug
out for her, knowing her too well. She hurried
back to the bedroom and set her laptop up on
the desk. Working to figure this out was the
only way to move past the grief.

She waited for her laptop to boot up. If she'd
needed more confirmation that Sarah had been
the main target, she'd just gotten it with the
break-in at Sarah's home. After the attempt on

her life on the river, she hadn't needed the confirmation, but she was glad Ryan now seemed convinced.

She realized now the burglar hadn't entered the home and waited for her return in order to kill her, the way the shooter on the river had. No. She'd stumbled upon a simple break-in. That left her confused about what was going on. But she feared that whoever had been searching the house might have gotten what they'd been looking for. If so, she wouldn't have that clue to know what had gotten Sarah killed.

Her laptop booted up, Tori pulled up the emails she'd received from Sarah. She never deleted an email, for which she was now grateful. She started reading as far back as she could retrieve the emails. Distance hadn't diminished Sarah's relationship with Tori, but Tori's job had prevented her from being as engaged as she should have been with her family.

Tears burned down her cheeks and she accepted they wouldn't be the last, as she continued to read, searching for that one email that could possibly give her a clue.

Her cell rang. Ryan. Her heart warmed with the thought of him—which aggravated her. She needed to stay focused on the case, not get distracted by an old flame. Still battling annoyance with herself, she answered, "What have you found?"

He snorted. "Can we back up to hello or hi or how are you?"

"Why waste time?" She leaned her forehead against her hand. "I'm sorry. Hi, Ryan. How are you?"

"That's more like it. Rough morning?"

"You could say that." She kept what had happened with her parents and their suggestion of moving to South Carolina to herself. "So, was this just a friendly call to check on me?"

She hoped not, though at the same time, she liked the idea.

"Yes and no. Now that I've checked on you, I have some news. First, your dad called me and asked me to keep the bungalow under crime-scene lockdown."

Dad! She sucked in a breath. "What?"

"He doesn't want you moving back there. I can't blame him. I advised you against it."

"So when do you think I can move back in?"

He exhaled loudly. "It's ready now. The crime scene techs worked late into the night and finished up this morning."

"I'm so glad. Did they find anything?"

"Time will tell, Tori. Please be patient. You know these things take a while."

"Right. Okay. Thanks for letting me know.

And thanks for releasing the crime scene. I'm going to move back to the bungalow. I need to be in town for Mom and Dad, be accessible to them, but living with them is…hard."

"I understand."

Ryan had three siblings and they, along with his parents, lived in the Mount Shasta region. Close enough to be together for important events, eat Sunday dinner or hang out, but not too close.

"It's worse now because they're smothering me." Tori squeezed her eyes shut. She hadn't meant to reveal so much of what was going on.

"Honestly, Tori, I don't blame them." The tone in his voice made her think he would like to do the same. But she must be hearing things.

"Thanks for calling to let me know."

"Wait, don't hang up yet," he said.

"Is there something else you want to tell me?"

"Yes. I'm standing at the front door."

After ending the call, Ryan stood at the front door waiting. He didn't want to knock or ring the bell and disturb her mother and father, especially after what Tori had just told him. Plus, they would ask questions for which he had no answers. Tori might do the same. She was taking her time answering the door. Maybe she had decided she wasn't going to open it, after all.

Just as he lifted the phone to text her, the door swung open.

Tori rushed out. "Okay, let's go."

She walked right past him without a glance. Her purse slung over her shoulder and her briefcase and small duffel at her side, she hurried down the sidewalk to stand next to his vehicle, which he'd parked at the curb.

"Wait." He held back a laugh as he caught up with her and opened the door for her. She tossed in her things. "Where are we going?"

"You're taking me to Sarah's."

That was what he had in mind. Sort of. He'd wanted her to look at the house to see if anything was missing. More than that, he'd wanted to see her.

He climbed into his vehicle on the driver's side and started it. "Aren't you even going to say goodbye?"

"To my parents? I already told them you were taking me back to Sarah's. That's all right, isn't it? It was providential that you showed up when you did. Really, I appreciate the ride, Ryan."

"You're welcome." Tori's car, or rather Sarah's car that Tori had been driving while staying here, remained parked at the bungalow. "As a matter of fact, I had hoped to take you there to have you walk through and see if anything obvious was missing."

He pulled away from the curb. Sarah's bungalow was only a couple of neighborhoods over—barely a mile away. Her home was in the same neighborhood as Ryan's and was actually only a few houses down.

"Why the big rush to get out of there?" He glanced over as he drove. She must have recently showered. He could still smell the shampoo. She was beautiful as always, but she looked like she hadn't slept well last night. That was understandable. He stifled the desire to reach over and grab her hand to reassure her.

"I didn't mean to come across like I was in a hurry to leave." Tori stared out the passenger window.

He took a right at the intersection. "You could have fooled me."

She blew out a breath. "Okay, well, maybe just a little. I love Mom and Dad, but they're pressuring me to leave town. They've even offered to come with me."

"You mean visit you?"

"They talked about moving to South Carolina."

Wow. He drove slowly down the street, passing his house on the way to Sarah's. "And you're not encouraging them with their plans."

She jerked her head to him. "Of course not. They aren't thinking clearly, Ryan. Once they have gotten past the initial grieving process, they'll realize that they don't truly want to leave their home or their friends. They'll realize that they cherish the memories of Sarah here. A permanent move would be a rash decision based on emotions."

"While I agree with you that they need time to grieve before they make such big decisions, maybe they need some new scenery, at least for a little while. Something that doesn't remind them so much of Sarah until they've grieved enough." He pulled to the curb in front of Sarah's bungalow as he said the words. Great timing. Seeing the bungalow gave him a sick feeling in his gut. He could use a change of scenery, too.

Sarah had painted her home a light grayish blue to brighten it up, though the huge windows and the cozy front porch did a great job of that already. But Sarah wasn't here anymore to enjoy the work she'd put into her home. He shifted into Park and turned in the seat, facing Tori to talk more about her parents.

"Thanks." Tori opened the door. She stepped out but leaned back in to grab her briefcase, duffel and purse, and then said, "You don't have to come in with me."

He quickly got out and rushed around to walk with her. "Oh, no, you don't. You're not getting rid of me so easily. After what happened the last time, I'm going to clear the house before you go inside. Then I'll walk with you to see if anything is missing. I want to be here when you look through it all."

"That's not necessary," she said and closed the car door. "I can always give you a call later if I notice something." Tori hiked up the sidewalk lugging her things.

Ryan caught up with her and tried to relieve her of the duffel. "You'll hurt your shoulder."

Grimacing, she relinquished the bag. "Thanks. You're probably right."

"You're welcome. Oh, by the way—" he reached inside his jacket and grabbed her gun that he'd tucked in a pocket, then handed it over "—Jerry said no prints. You can have your weapon back. But I'm still going in first. Don't argue."

Ryan unlocked and opened the door. "Wait here in the foyer for me. You might try using the alarm next time. Turn it on when you leave but also while you're here in the house. If you'd armed it maybe the perp would have been deterred."

"I didn't know the code before, but Dad gave it to me this morning. But you and I both know he could disarm the alarm if he set his mind to it. You can learn how with an online tutorial."

Ryan frowned. "Then if you're going to stay here, we should get you set up with a state-of-the-art system."

"We?" she arched a brow.

Ryan didn't respond to her jab at his intrusion in the details of her life. Instead, he drew his weapon and moved through the home to make sure no one else had broken in. "Make sure to call for the window replacement today!" he called over his shoulder.

"Dad already did," she yelled from the foyer.

They were so familiar with each other. Maybe he was too close to this investigation, getting too involved with Tori, but he didn't think so. He was a professional and could compartmentalize his past relationship with her while he investigated Sarah's murder and the obviously related attacks on Tori.

After Ryan cleared the house, he found her dutifully waiting in the foyer, which surprised him.

Arms crossed, again she arched a brow—and a lovely, well-defined brow, at that. "Well? Find anyone suspicious?"

He tucked his weapon away. She would already know if he had. "Funny." He lifted her duffel, but she held her briefcase close. "Where do you want me to put this?"

"On the bed in the master bedroom. Sarah's room." Anxiety edged her words.

He moved down the hallway with Tori on his heels, glad she'd allowed him to help her if only a little. Her shoulder must be still be bothering her.

In Sarah's warmly decorated room, a pang struck his heart. He could only imagine what sleeping in her sister's room would do to Tori. When given the choice, Tori had chosen the guest bedroom to begin with. Interesting that the burglar hadn't been in Sarah's room searching but had instead been in the room where Tori was staying. He would keep that tidbit to himself for the time being.

He set the duffel on Sarah's bed, grief weighing on him. When he turned to face Tori, he caught her staring at the photographs neatly hung on the wall.

"Might as well start here," he said. "See anything missing?"

"I haven't been in her room yet. I... I was avoiding this moment, and now I'm in here looking at her stuff under completely different circumstances than I'd imagined. I thought I'd be packing up her things, not looking for anything that might be missing so we can figure out who broke in and if he's her killer."

He held back a sigh. "I know it's hard. You can do this."

She drew in a breath and stood taller, then gave him a look that said he needed to dial the reassurances and platitudes down. "I know I can do it, Ryan."

Her way of telling him she didn't need his encouragement. Or rather, she didn't want it. He wanted to argue that everyone needed encouragement, especially under circumstances like these, but he doubted Tori would be willing to listen. She prided herself too much on her ability to stand on her own two feet.

She didn't stay in Sarah's room long. He followed her through the house as she gave everything a once-over and then they ended up in the attic. Sarah had filled it with a few old boxes—memorabilia from school—but that was all.

Finally Tori finished her search in the kitchen. She shrugged. "I didn't see anything missing, but that doesn't mean it isn't."

Her staying in this house didn't sit well with him. "Look, are you sure you want to stay?"

She nodded. "If there's something to be discovered here, I'll find it by staying."

He wouldn't convince her otherwise. "Before

I leave, I'll board up the broken window until you can get the glass replaced."

"Thanks, Ryan, but Dad is coming over this afternoon to do that now that you've released the scene."

"Oh, right. Okay." He squeezed the keys in his pocket—Sarah's house keys that he should give back to Tori. But he held on to them for now. "At least give your parents' suggestion a thought. Go back to your job. Years ago, you couldn't wait to get out of here. Remember? Go back and let your parents come and visit with you for a while, and then see what happens. If they move, they move. There's nothing you can do about that. But you'll all be safer there." And if she left, then she wouldn't be staying in this house. She wouldn't be here in northern California to be targeted again.

"Are you kidding me? My job there keeps me busy around the clock." She shook her head. "I wouldn't have time for them."

"Maybe it would be a good idea to be back at work so you can get your mind on other matters." And let him solve this. But he was hoping for too much.

"That's not going to happen. I can't stop thinking about finding who killed Sarah." She opened the fridge. "You want a soda or something?"

He let his gaze roam through the kitchen,

dining and living area again. He knew this whole house well by now, after spending last night searching for a clue in the quaint home.

Ryan suddenly realized Tori was staring at him, Coke in hand. He took it, though he wasn't really thirsty. "I know I can't stop you from doing your own investigation. But remember, you're not even a licensed private investigator. This isn't an FBI investigation."

"Get real."

"Exactly. I'm under no illusion that you're going to stop. I'm only going to ask you to be careful. You could ruin my investigation. Mess with evidence. Keep me from putting this person away."

She came across to plop on the sofa with her Coke. "Don't worry, you and I will be investigating on very different paths."

He fisted his hands. "Still think you're going to find this killer on your own while I'm off on a wild-goose chase?"

Opening her laptop, she popped the Coke top, and fizz nearly overflowed to her computer.

"Careful!" He quickly snatched a towel from her kitchen and tossed it her way.

"Thanks." She cleaned up the mess, drank the Coke and eyed him. "You've got it all wrong."

"My investigation is not even good enough to

be on your radar, is that it?" Could he just shut up? Why did she seem to push all the wrong buttons? Or right buttons, depending on one's perspective.

"It's not a question of your skills or abilities. I just have insight into Sarah that you can't match. I'm going to walk in her steps in a way you and your team could never do. That's all."

He shoved his hands in his pockets. "Fine. Make sure you share with me when you find something."

"You've already told me that I'm not on your team."

He sighed and softened his next words. "Let's put aside our…competition, for lack of a better word… And find Sarah's killer before he can get away."

To his surprise, Tori set her Coke on the coffee table, the other end from her laptop, and moved to stand next to him.

He could tell by the haunted look in her eyes that sadness still clung to her heart, but determination remained there, too. Good. He wouldn't expect to see anything less in her gaze. Those dark green irises could still hold him captive. Tori stood close and he caught another whiff of her coconut shampoo. Her face was clean and free of makeup. She was beautiful just like this.

"Thank you, Ryan. For being here for me. For being there for Sarah. I started reading through her emails and she mentioned how you helped a few times when her car broke down. Or she needed to borrow something. You made her feel safe."

He shrugged, grief strangling him. "Just doing my duty."

"It was more than that, and you know it. You were kind of like a big brother to her." He'd treated Sarah like a little sister when he and Tori had been together before. And he hadn't stopped just because Tori had broken his heart.

It hit him that Tori was all alone now. Where he had three siblings, she'd lost the only sibling she had.

He wasn't sure how it happened, but Tori was suddenly wrapped in his arms. It felt right and good for all the reasons it shouldn't. He knew better than to think anything lasting could come of this. Still, they'd shared a bond once, and now that bond had moved to one of deep loss. He wished he could hold her for as long as it took for the pain to leave them both. Wished he could convince her to go to the safety of South Carolina, or that she'd become willing to believe that he could solve this—that he wouldn't let her down. But that was all fantasy.

And Ryan lived in the real world.

She stepped away from his embrace and stood taller as she wiped her eyes. "I'm sorry."

"You don't have to be." Tenderness coursed through him. He wanted to pull her back in his arms. He wished they could turn back time and have another go at a life together. Maybe Sarah could still be here with them, too, if he was going to wish for impossible things.

"We both have work to do, Ryan." She opened the door and effectively dismissed him.

FIVE

He almost looked hurt. "Be sure to set the alarm."

"I will." Tori couldn't exactly slam the door in his face, so she waited for him to walk away.

He held her gaze for a moment longer, then turned and walked down the sidewalk. She watched him until he got into his vehicle and then, finally, he drove away.

Tori closed the door, locked it and dutifully set the alarm. Then she remembered the window. She headed to the room where she'd slept while here and saw that the techs had at least put plastic over the window. The frame was still in place—funny the alarm was armed but she had a gaping hole in her house, for all practical purposes.

She grabbed her cell and texted her father to ask when he would be over to board it up. She could do it herself, except her shoulder still hurt. Plus, she knew her father and he would be hurt if she didn't allow him this one small gesture of help.

Dad texted back that he was at the hardware store and would be by the house later in the day. She loved her parents so much and was glad that she could be close to them at this difficult time—just not *too* close. They each needed space to grieve in their own way. And her way of grieving was working to find Sarah's murderer. She needed to help Ryan. She settled on the sofa and set her weapon on the side table, glad to have it back.

Finally she could focus—at least until Dad got here. She concentrated on reading through Sarah's emails to her over the last several years.

It seemed like a long shot, but it was a good start. Some of them, she'd forgotten completely. She snacked on Doritos and chocolate and guzzled more sodas—almost as if she and Sarah were hanging out. Laughing and crying together.

Her cell buzzed. Mom. She texted her back that she'd be over for pot roast this evening but couldn't come over early since she was busy at the moment and also was waiting on Dad to fix the window.

Her phone buzzed again. Only this time it was a call from Ryan. She pursed her lips. She didn't trust her voice to sound steady just now.

She texted him that she was all right, on the off chance he was calling to check up on her.

He wasn't much better than her parents when it came to the smothering, and that thought sent odd and yet familiar sensations through her.

I have work to do. She pushed thoughts of Ryan away to focus on the emails.

One email sent only two months ago made mention of an issue regarding land pollution. Sarah had said she was heading to Sacramento, California's capital, to protest. Tori sat up. With this email, she might be getting somewhere. Sarah had always been about social justice issues as well as environmental causes. Following this small clue could lead her nowhere, but Tori had to start somewhere. Though there were more emails to read, she could get back to those after a little digging on this.

After researching online, she finally found the name of a guy who had organized a protest in Sacramento over an agricultural pesticide used on commercial farms. The event had taken place around the same time as Sarah's email. Tori decided to go with it.

The guy's name was Dee James and he headed up an organization called A Better World.

It wouldn't hurt to call him to ask if he knew Sarah. Tori searched through online databases until she found the person she believed was the right man, though she couldn't be sure. There were a few listings under that name. She would try them all if that was what it took.

And in fact, she was able to narrow it down to three different Dee Jameses.

She left a voice mail for each of them.

If one of these numbers was his, he probably wasn't picking up because he didn't recognize her number. She gave him a few minutes to call her back or at least listen to the voice mail. If one of the men knew Sarah, maybe they would call back. Tori was counting on it. She needed to find something. She needed a win.

Someone knocked on the door. Tori grabbed her weapon and peeked through the peephole to see her father. She let him in just as her cell rang.

"I need to take this, Dad. Go ahead and work on the window." She smiled and then looked at the phone. Her heart jumped. Maybe it was him. "Hello? Dee James?"

An intake of breath. "Yes. I'm returning your call."

"Thanks. As I mentioned in my voice mail, I'm Tori Peterson. I'm Sarah's sister."

A few breaths of quiet, then he said, "I'm sorry for your loss."

Of course, he already knew about the death.

"Yes, well, thank you." Tori cleared her throat. "I was hoping you could help me."

Again, he was silent for a few heartbeats. This man was wary.

"I don't know how," he finally said.

"Can you meet me to talk? I'll buy you a cup of coffee." If she could get him in person she could read his expression. Plus, he might be willing to share information—that is, if he had any.

"I don't know anything about what happened to Sarah. I'm sorry, but you're wasting your time if you think I can help."

"But you were in an environmental group with her, right?"

"Yeah, so? She was in lots of groups with lots of people."

Ah. Now. So she was getting somewhere. He knew enough about Sarah to know that. Still, she had the feeling he wasn't going to agree to meet her. So she had to press her point and see how he reacted. "I read some information about suspicious activities such as…um…ecoterrorism. The FBI was checking into that. I… I just want to find out if Sarah was involved with the group, that's all."

"You already know she was involved in A Better World, and as I mentioned, many more groups besides."

Tori was going to lose him and soon. She was surprised he'd stayed on the line this long. Maybe he feared if he didn't satisfy her that she wouldn't go away. "Yes, well, I mean, was Sarah involved in any suspicious or violent activities? I'm not trying to build a case. I just want to know why someone would try to kill her."

Dad's hammering echoed through the house and she tried to concentrate on Dee's words. "I don't know anything about any suspicious activities. I'm sorry for what happened to Sarah, but I don't know anything to help." He ended the call.

Tori stared at the cell. Her mouth went dry. The call had the kind of tension that let her know she was on to something here. Dee James probably regretted returning her call. He'd probably thought he could brush her off and make her go away. Now he would be worried and maybe even try to flee—that is, if he had something to hide.

The unnatural tension in his voice told her that he did.

Dad emerged from the hallway. "All done."

"What? That was fast."

"The window should be restored tomorrow afternoon."

"Thanks, Dad." She smiled.

"I can see you're busy. Will your mother and I see you later?"

Tori didn't want to lose her momentum after that conversation with Dee. "I'll be at dinner. We can talk more then." She got up, moved to her father and kissed him on the cheek. "Thanks, Dad. I'll see you tonight, okay?"

"Okay." She knew him well enough to see he had more to say, but she was grateful when he kept it to himself and bade her goodbye. He let himself out. She reset the alarm and got back to work.

Thunder rumbled through the house. She made notes of her conversation and then read through more emails, carefully now. If she'd been reading too fast, she would have missed the mention of the environmental protest, though she should have known to look into that to begin with. There had to be a ton of environmental groups in the area. She would make a list of the groups and the major participants, but she was pretty sure Dee James was someone to question further and she would make sure to do that soon.

The sound of torrential rain soon followed.

Then, the power went out. Of course! After what had happened here, staying alone in the darkened bungalow was too creepy, and since she couldn't continue her internet search, Tori decided to head out.

She wrote down an address she'd found for this Dee James and then she shut down her laptop. She might as well make use of the downtime.

After grabbing a light jacket and an umbrella, she ran to the car but was drenched even though she'd used her umbrella. The issue came when she tried to close her umbrella and tuck it inside the vehicle. Tori wiped the water from her face and smoothed her hair. Maybe she should have waited until the rain stopped but that was a moot point now. She turned on the vehicle and activated the windshield wipers.

Though she probably shouldn't head out in the storm, sitting in Sarah's house without power wasn't a safe option, either. She thought of Ryan and his investigation.

See, I told you, we wouldn't even cross paths.

No way was he following this particular lead. He needed Tori on this and didn't even know it.

She thought back to the moment when he held her. Of them holding each other. They had been grieving together over Sarah, but there had been something more between them. Tender emotions that had nothing to do with Sarah's death. A knot lodged in her throat. She pushed those unbidden thoughts away.

It was much too late for them, and she couldn't think about that.

She had to think about her sister.

Sarah, what did you get yourself into?

Ryan trudged down the hallway in the Maynor County Sheriff's Office, feeling the effects of a long day in which he'd learned nothing new.

"Any news, Bradley?" Sheriff Rollins asked, calling to him from his office at the far end of the hallway. Ryan's direct boss was Captain Moran, who was in charge of the investigations division. Above Captain Moran was Chief Deputy Carmichael, who oversaw the patrol, court and investigations divisions. But the sheriff, who headed up the entire department, took a special interest in this case. The multiple homicide had drawn much attention and he wanted the case solved expeditiously. Ryan wanted a promotion, and he knew he'd better handle and solve this case or he could kiss any chance of that goodbye.

Sheriff Rollins headed toward him, change jingling in his pocket. Ryan scraped a hand down his face. He hadn't yet shared with his boss, Captain Moran, that he was leaning toward Sarah being the primary target. Sheriff Rollins still believed the Mason kid's years-old drug involvement had spurred the homicides. Ryan had spent the day trying to close up those loose ends before he could present his theory to Moran in a way that couldn't be doubted or ignored. He didn't like disclosing this to the sheriff without Moran weighing in. After measuring his response, he opened his mouth to speak—

"Ryan?" Hope Rollins was the office receptionist and the sheriff's niece.

He turned to see Hope approaching him. "Sarah Peterson's father, David, is here. He wants to speak to you."

The sheriff's cell buzzed. He gave Ryan a harried look. "Go ahead. You can add this conversation with Mr. Peterson into your reports. We'll talk tomorrow."

Ryan hoped he hid his relief and turned to the receptionist. "I'll get him. Is the conference room available?"

"I'll check. If not, I'll find you another room."

What could the man want besides answers Ryan didn't have? He buzzed through the door into the lobby. "Mr. Peterson, come on back."

The man barely smiled. "No need for formalities with me, son. We've been through too much for that. You can call me David."

He'd prefer the formalities while at his place

of employment, but he didn't want to argue. Saying nothing, Ryan offered a tenuous smile and led the man to the conference room. He gestured to a chair. "Coffee? Water?"

"Nothing for me, thanks. I would have called you, but I wanted to have this conversation in person."

"I could have stopped by the house. I don't live that far from you."

"I didn't want Sheryl to know that I talked to you. Or Tori, for that matter. She's coming over for dinner tonight, by the way." His eyes brightened with the words, if only slightly. "Please join us, if you like."

"Mr. Peterson. Um… David, please tell me what's on your mind. Have you remembered something about Sarah that could help the investigation?"

David clasped his hands and hesitated, then finally said, "This is about Tori, not Sarah."

Ryan had figured as much. "Go on."

"Her mother and I, we don't want her to stay here. I can't lose another daughter."

Ryan measured his words. He wanted Tori to go, as well, but he had to tread carefully here and not get into the middle of a family disagreement. "I'm confused. How can I help?"

"I'm hoping as a detective you can discourage her from trying to find Sarah's killer, that's how. Isn't there something you can do to keep her out of the investigation? If she can't look into things, she has no reason to stay."

Ah. "There's nothing I can do to stop her. I've already tried to talk her out of it. She's determined to find the killer. All I can do is keep her close. Work with her as much as possible."

David crossed his arms and leaned back in the chair. "We need her to be safe. What can we do?"

"Maybe she needs *you*," Ryan said. "She needs the familiarity of her home and the people she loves."

"We've thought of that. That's why we offered to move with her. Or at least visit her where she lives in South Carolina for months, however long is necessary."

Ryan's heart went out to the man. There were no easy answers. "What you need is a therapist or a counselor. Someone who can help you all work through this time of grief. I take it you're not seeing one."

He shrugged. "Even thinking about that… it just hurts too much. We don't want to talk about our feelings with a stranger."

Ryan refrained from scraping a hand down his face. "I'll talk to Tori, but you know she probably won't listen to me."

"Thank you. And, son, you have more influence over her than you know, despite what happened in the past. She still admires you and I believe she'll listen to you." David blew out a breath, relief apparent on his face.

As if Ryan alone could make Tori change her mind. David was about to be disappointed.

"I'll give it a try," Ryan said. "Was there anything else?"

"No. That's it." David stood. "I appreciate you taking a few minutes to listen."

Ryan was surprised David didn't ask if they had made any progress on Sarah's murder case. "Of course. I'll walk you out."

After Tori's father had gone, Ryan headed to his cubicle. He still needed to finish writing up his reports, but that would have to wait. He rubbed his eyes. He'd already tried to call Tori this afternoon and she was ignoring his calls. She'd texted him to let him know she was okay, so at least there was that.

He needed to maintain his emotional distance while still keeping his finger on the pulse of her little private investigation. The other side of the equation—he hadn't been able to stop thinking about her since she'd returned. Opening a drawer, he slammed it shut to vent his frustration with himself, earning a few looks from his fellow county employees. How had he gotten to this place in his life? He thought he had finally moved on from her but instead, he was right back to square one. It made no sense!

He exited the county offices and got in his vehicle. If she wasn't answering, he should check up on her.

The sky had been gray and rainy this afternoon and he turned the windshield wipers to the highest setting as he steered through town toward home. He would stop by the bungalow first; he hoped she was there and not out in this weather.

To his surprise, Tori steered right past him, going in the opposite direction.

Ryan made a quick U-turn in the middle of the highway as he grumbled under his breath, although he didn't know why he bothered to keep his voice low. He was alone in his vehicle as he followed Tori.

She would be furious when she found out he'd tailed her. *If* she found out.

Following her hadn't been his intention, but she'd ignored his call, choosing to text him a short message instead. And her father had paid him a visit.

Still, the investigation into the multiple homicides needed to be his top priority, not Tori herself. But after the two attempts on her life, he remained concerned about her safety. And she was tangled up in this investigation whether he liked it or not.

The rain wasn't helping matters. His windshield wipers couldn't keep up with the torrent.

Tori drove out of town and just kept driving along the freeway. What business could she have out here? Tension built up in his shoulders as he followed Tori for a good forty-five minutes, and she never noticed him on her tail—he could thank the weather for that.

In Shady Creek, Tori parked her vehicle at the curb near a cluster of apartments. Across the street was a laundromat, an insurance office and a coffee shop advertising free internet. The downpour continued as if the storm had traveled with them to the next town. The rain had probably ceased in Rainey—he laughed out loud at that. But in Shady Creek, the storm kept up.

Shady Creek was in Maynor County, so it was still part of his jurisdiction, but if she'd gone as far as Shasta County he would have continued to follow her as part of this investigation.

She'd learned something. He knew it. But what?

The thought soured in his stomach. He thought they had an understanding and had agreed that she would share whatever she learned so that he could more quickly find the murderer. He parked across the street from where she'd parked and noticed she had remained in her vehicle so far. He was down a ways, too, and needed to think through his next steps. Should he follow her from a distance or should he make his presence known? If he did reveal himself, would she be forthcoming with what she'd discovered?

Though it was still raining, Tori got out of her vehicle, wearing a hooded jacket. She started down the sidewalk of the quiet two-way street.

Ryan tugged his wind jacket on and pulled the hood up. Looked like he was getting out in the rain, too. Hoodie covering his head, he tried to follow her. He decided that once he knew her destination, he'd make his presence known. Unfortunately, he wasn't certain she would give up what she knew, even though he was the detective on the case.

Unease crept up his spine and his senses kicked into high gear.

Something wasn't right. Call it instinct or a gut feeling, but he'd learned to never ignore it.

Tugging her jacket tighter, Tori glanced over her shoulder at the slow traffic as if to rush across the street. She started across and Ryan made to cut her off, done with trailing her.

An engine revved behind them as a vehicle rushed forward, heading directly for Tori.

"Look out!"

SIX

The grille of the blue crossover filled Ryan's peripheral vision as he propelled himself forward. Tori twisted around as he grabbed her. Gripping her arms, he dove with her out of the vehicle's path. Together they slammed against the sidewalk, though Ryan rolled to absorb the bulk of the impact. Pain stabbed through him, but he ignored it.

Protecting her, he held her on top, his back against the asphalt. Tires squealed as the vehicle sped away. Gasping, he tried to jerk his gaze around to catch the license plate, but he couldn't see it as it turned the corner. Still, he had the make and model. He would radio the information in for law enforcement to be on the lookout.

Would the vehicle come back? Had the near collision been intentional or had he overreacted? He didn't think he had.

As if it hadn't been pouring hard enough, the

ground began to crackle with drops. The rain wouldn't give them a break.

"Ryan!" Tori's voice startled him.

He'd been focused on the vehicle and only now realized she'd been calling his name. She stared down at him. "You can let me go now."

What? Oh, he still gripped her tightly to him. "Are you all right? Are you hurt?"

"No, I'm not all right." Her dark green eyes pierced him. Her frown deepened. "What are you doing here?"

"Saving you, apparently." He opened his hands, releasing her.

She got to her feet, then offered her hand to assist him up. Her grip was slick with rain and his hand slipped free, but he got to his feet anyway.

"I'm good." Was he? His back might never be the same, and for sure he'd have a few bruises. But rushing Tori out of the way had been worth it. No doubt there.

He glanced around them. Was someone else watching and waiting? The rain kept everyone inside, and if someone had witnessed what happened, no one had stopped to help them.

"I don't understand. Why are you here?" Water droplets beaded on her weather-resistant hoodie.

"Let's get out of the rain and go somewhere

safe and dry," he said. "Maybe you can tell me where you were going."

Hands on her hips, she angled her head. "And you can tell me why you were following me."

"You know, it's kind of hard to have a meaningful conversation in this downpour." He offered a grin to defuse the tension.

"Come on." She took his hand, and they rushed over to the café across the street.

Tori stepped through the glass door first and a jingle announced their presence. The small internet café was empty except for an employee—the barista—arranging mugs. The space felt warm and welcoming, and the aroma of fresh coffee filled the air.

The barista glanced up and waved them over. "What'll it be? And it's on the house."

"Really?" Ryan angled his head.

"Sure. You two look like you could use a free cup of joe today."

Tori chuckled.

Ryan's shoes squeaked as he made his way to the counter. He glanced at the menu, his mind on anything but coffee. "A regular coffee for me."

"Cappuccino macchiato for me." Shivering, Tori hugged herself.

"Give me a minute to make a call." Ryan

tugged out his cell, grateful it had remained dry, and moved to stand by the glass storefront.

He stared at the gray sky's relentless payload while he made his call. Would he see the vehicle again? Was someone following Tori— someone *else*? He contacted dispatch and reported the type of vehicle that had tried to run her down. He didn't think he'd mistaken the vehicle's intent. Still, without a license plate there wasn't much more to go on. Deputies could be on the lookout in the area and they would go from there.

When he ended the call, he turned his attention back to the café and spotted Tori in a booth against the wall, a fusion of bar towels wrapped around her. She'd taken off the jacket, which hadn't exactly been waterproof enough for this deluge. The blue T-shirt she wore was soaked. He approached and smiled down.

"The guy was really nice." She gripped the mug with both hands to warm herself. "He brought me this towel and is bringing some more. Said business had been slow today."

"I'd think more people would be here getting coffee in this weather," he said.

She shrugged and sipped on her cappuccino. He slid into the booth, next to her, forcing her to scoot over, then reached over to grab his plain coffee placed across the booth.

"What are you doing?" She scooted closer to the wall. "You're supposed to sit across from me."

His preference, too. "I can't see the door from that side. Would you like to sit over there instead?"

"No. Then *my* back would be to the door."

"Then I guess you're stuck with me sitting here."

Weren't they a cute law enforcement pair? Except they weren't a couple at all. Still, sitting next to her like this, he could almost pretend they were. But he would steer clear from thoughts like that.

"Actually, now that you're here, I could use your warmth. You can stay." She smiled. "For now."

"Funny. You do realize that I'm blocking your escape. You have to go through me to get out."

She arched a brow. "Is that a challenge?"

He chuckled. *What am I doing sitting here with Tori and laughing?* "No."

There was a killer out there. At least one. Maybe more than one. He took a swig of the hot coffee and focused on the situation.

Ryan stared out the window, watching for any other anomalies. Anyone else who might want to hurt Tori. He let the anger of the situation sober him. He needed something to create resistance to the warmth he could feel coming off her.

Tori positioned herself at an angle against the wall so she was half facing him, half facing the table. He felt her green eyes on him but continued to watch out the window. He almost wanted the driver to come back so he could detain him. Or her. He honestly didn't know if it had been a female or a male.

Then again, maybe they shouldn't stay long enough for whoever it was to come back. It might be better if he ushered Tori home. She didn't seem to realize that someone had just tried to kill her. Again.

Or maybe she didn't want to accept it.

"What happened back there?" she asked.

He turned to look at her. The wet ends of her hair were finally drying.

"Why were you following me?" Tori stared at him over the rim of her mug.

"I wasn't *exactly* following you."

"Oh, yeah, what would you call it? You showed up here. How did you get here if you didn't follow me?"

"You didn't answer my call, for one."

"No, but I texted you that I was okay."

"After what happened, I wanted to make sure that was true. For all I knew, someone else could have stolen your phone and sent that message. I headed home and thought I'd stop in to make sure you were all right, plus find out if you learned anything today. You sped right past me. So yeah, maybe I turned around to see where you were going." He'd leave her father out of it for the moment. She had enough issues going with her parents.

"And followed me."

Ignoring her indignation, Ryan watched the slow traffic through the big plate glass window. Time to redirect her. "Why don't we focus on the more serious issue? You haven't said one thing to me or asked me about why I pushed you out of the way. Did you realize that someone tried to run you over?"

He turned to see her reaction. Her face paled and she shifted her position. She was entirely too close.

"I thought… I thought I had somehow stepped out in front of a car. I didn't realize… Are you sure?"

"Yes. It caught me off guard, too, but I was approaching you to make my presence known when I heard the engine rev and the vehicle pulled from the curb and headed straight for you. I yelled for you to look out."

"I turned to see who was yelling."

"I didn't have time to explain. I only had

time to shove you out of the way. Didn't you hear the vehicle speeding up?"

She stared into her cappuccino macchiato. He knew that admitting that she hadn't been aware of someone following or targeting her would be hard for her. She hadn't even known that Ryan was following her. He suspected Sarah's death was clouding her mind and impacting her usual perceptiveness. More now that she realized Sarah had been the intended target. The grief and stress were pressing in on her. That was why a bereavement leave was given. But instead of using this time to cope with her loss and work through her feelings, Tori refused to give herself time to process Sarah's murder. He wouldn't press her on what she'd missed today, but there was something else he would press her on.

"So, what's here? Why did you come to Shady Creek? I have a feeling you're following a lead."

She had hoped he wouldn't go there. "Back up. I'm still reeling over the fact you claimed someone tried to run me over."

Tori squeezed the bridge of her nose and took a breath. What was the matter with her? If what Ryan said was true and someone had tried to run her down, then this latest attack meant that two people had been following her and she'd missed that. Or one person had followed her and one had waited for her here. Either way, she was getting careless. Her hand shook as she tried to lift the now tepid drink to her lips.

Ryan still waited for an answer to his question and Tori wasn't ready to give him one. She eyed him over the rim of her cup. She wished she had opted for sitting across from him now. He was much too close.

She tried to shake off the effect his nearness was having on her. How had she found herself so close to him twice in one day? She shivered again, the still-damp clothes fighting against her attempts to get warm. She almost wished she could lean into Ryan and soak up some of his body heat, but she was drawn to him for other reasons, too. Reasons she wouldn't indulge.

But he was waiting on an answer. "Clearly, I didn't make it to the place where I could learn something, as you put it."

"Come on, Tori. You know we'll get to the bottom of this faster if we work together."

"As soon as I know anything solid, I'll share it." She angled her head to look at him. She knew a little but it was mostly a feeling she was going on here. "I don't have any facts worth your time."

He worked his strong jaw back and forth. His slicked-back hair was now mussed, even though he'd tried to shove it back into place. His blue-green eyes held both appreciation and… something more. Affection. Getting a glimpse of that sent longing coursing through her. And she absolutely couldn't act on any part of that. She couldn't afford to miss what she once had with this man, or think about how much she wished she hadn't had to make a choice between him and a career she'd wanted.

The barista—Tom—approached the table, interrupting her thoughts. "Some more towels if you like. They're just small dish towels, but they're dry."

"Thank you, Tom," Tori said. She didn't want to reach over Ryan to take them. "That's very kind of you."

He set them on the table, smiled and left. She wished he would bring her another cappuccino macchiato.

As if he weren't close enough, Ryan leaned closer to Tori after Tom left. "I think he's a great guy, but he's also looking for a big tip since there are so few customers today."

Tori smiled. "I think he deserves one."

Ryan smiled back and held her gaze for a few breaths. "Me, too."

"Maybe we should leave that tip and get out

of here." Tori needed to escape her proximity to Ryan.

"I had hoped that whoever tried to run you over might come back." They had either followed her and had parked when she parked, or had been lying in wait for her.

"Oh, really." She feigned outrage.

"Yes. We could get a license plate. A face. Something to find out who is behind this." He guzzled the rest of his coffee and set the empty cup on the table.

"But now you want to leave?" She did, too, but if she could keep him talking about something else, she might be able to prevent him from pursuing information about why she'd come to Shady Creek. She didn't want to share too much. At least, not yet. If she got Ryan involved too early then she'd stand no chance of getting more information out of Dee James. James knew something.

"Yes. The towels aren't doing enough to warm you up."

"And how do you know that?"

"Your lips are still kind of blue." His gaze lingered on her lips.

Tori's heart skipped erratically. She needed to escape from where he'd purposefully pinned her so he could protect her. While he'd been serious about not sitting with his back to the door, she was sure protecting her was the real reason he'd sat beside her. She knew that much about Ryan.

The thought stirred her heart and made her miss him and what she'd left behind all the more.

"Okay, then, let's get out of here." After all, if she couldn't lean against him to get warmer, she needed to get home so she could get out of the wet clothes. Her jeans hadn't dried at all and the cold and wet chilled her to the core.

She'd have to come back to talk to Dee James another time. Ryan and Tori both pulled bills out and left them on the table for a more than adequate tip, and thanked the barista.

At the glass doors, Ryan tugged her aside. "Be careful. I'll walk you to your car and stay with you until you get in. Then I'll follow you home."

She gave him a wry grin. "I wouldn't expect any less of you." She still wasn't entirely sure how she felt about the way that he'd been following her at all, not counting the fact that she'd missed her tail completely to begin with.

The rain had slowed while they were in the café but now it came down in sheets again. "Really? It's like it was just waiting for us to finish our coffee. Can we run?"

He frowned and subtly shook his head. "I've

got a bad feeling that I can't explain. I got that right before the vehicle went for you. Let's take mine instead. I'll send deputies to bring yours back."

"What? No, that's not going to work for me." Tori reached into her bag to dig for her keys.

When she glanced up, Ryan's eyes had widened.

Tori turned in time to see the grille of a vehicle heading right toward them!

As if in slow motion, she and Ryan gripped hands and ran toward the back of the building. He yelled at Tom. "Get away. Move out of the way!"

Tom looked up, startled, and then his expression filled with horror. He dropped the glass mugs he was holding and then ran to the door that led to the kitchen. He opened the door and waved them in. "In here! Come in here!"

The vehicle crashed through the plate glass window and it shattered behind them as the engine revved and the ceiling crumbled. Tori and Ryan ducked as they ran forward and propelled themselves through the door that Tom held open for them.

Tori feared their efforts to escape wouldn't be enough as the three of them kept running, continuing to the back of the kitchen. Tom held another door wide for them that opened up to the alley behind the strip of buildings. Still running, they rushed outside and into the rain.

Ryan got on his cell and called emergency services and then the local police, as well as the sheriff's department, to let them know his version of what happened, all while he peered at her. Done with his business, he tucked his cell away.

"I need to check on the driver," he said. "But I also need to keep you safe."

"I'm going with you to see who was driving," she said.

Ryan scowled.

To Tom, he said, "Sorry we brought trouble to your workplace, Tom. Please hang around so we can take your statement."

"Cool, man. I'm sorry this happened, too."

"Please don't go back inside the building."

"I can just wait in my car. It's over there." He pointed to a small gray sedan parked in the alley.

"Okay. Someone will come for you to take your statement, if you want to wait there."

Ryan started jogging around the building.

She followed him around to the front to get a better look at the damage.

"It's not stable," he said. "I don't want you anywhere near that building."

She peered inside without going in. "I don't see anyone in the car."

"He or she could be unconscious, but I think you're right. The door is open. Looks like the perp fled."

"Was this the car you said tried to run me over?"

Frowning, he nodded.

"Ryan?" Tori sniffed. "I smell gas. Do you think the crash severed a gas line?"

He tugged her across the street as a concussive force slammed into them and drove them forward.

SEVEN

Ryan weighed her down. Once again he'd protected her. She was grateful, but she also couldn't breathe. She pushed against him and squirmed.

"Ryan, I'm okay." She croaked out. "Can you let me up now? We have to quit doing this."

"Funny. And no, I don't ever want to let you up again."

"Stop joking. This isn't the time. I... I can't breathe."

He crawled from her, stood and assisted her up as he looked her up and down. "Are you okay? Did the blast hurt you?"

She sucked in a few gasps for breath. "No, I don't think so. You knocked the air from me, that's all." Or the blast had done that, but if that was the case, she would have some organ damage, too, except she felt okay. It wasn't the blast but Ryan's protective nature that had caused the minor issue.

Concern and regret filled his features. "I didn't hurt you, did I?"

Despite the dire circumstances, Tori offered him a soft smile. "I'll probably be sporting a few bruises tomorrow—" she glanced across the street "—but those are nothing compared to what Tom's café will look like after the fire is done with it." Flames shot through the front and licked the roof. The insurance office next to the café didn't have any noticeable damage yet, but the structures could be unstable. Still, they were far enough away that they could be all right.

Ryan's cell rang and he answered, but he kept a grip on her arm.

A crowd started to gather, probably including the insurance staff, those in the laundromat and people who lived in the apartment complex. Was Dee James among them? Early on, she'd searched for his picture and found him—a red-headed guy in his late twenties. But she didn't see him among those watching the explosion.

Of course the rain had stopped right when it could have been useful dousing the fire. She shook her head, unable to understand the weather or the events that led up to this moment.

Sorrow and anger gutted her. Could the café be in flames because she and Ryan had chosen to drink a cup of coffee in there? She covered her mouth to hold back sobs. Reminded herself she was an FBI agent and needed to act the part. And as an agent on leave, here unofficially, she wanted to help. But how?

The best help she could offer at the moment was to get out of here. Ryan needed to focus on this situation and not hover around her to protect her.

When he ended the call, she said, "Ryan, you need to do your job and I need to leave. I'm just going to go home."

Instead of letting her go, he gripped both of her arms and turned her to face him. Tori wanted to shrug free, but the pure terror in his eyes kept her frozen.

"You need to take this threat on your life more seriously. Sure, you're trained and know how to protect yourself, but have you ever had someone actively trying to kill you? Someone who is relentless in seeking you out?"

Her mouth suddenly went dry. "No. You're right. This is…this is different."

"You probably need to tell your superiors about these attacks, if they don't already know." He rubbed a hand down his face. "In the meantime, you're not taking your car home today. You're riding with me. I'll take you home. We already decided that, remember?"

"That was before the explosion. You're needed here now."

Ryan ignored her comment and took her hand, kept her closer than she would have liked as they hurried down the sidewalk. He led her over to his vehicle. Opened the door for her and waited as she climbed in. Fire trucks and other emergency vehicles had arrived and were blocking the street.

"What about Tom? Don't you need to go get his statement?" she asked.

Before he could reply, a fireman headed for Ryan, who'd repositioned his badge to hang around his neck so it was visible. Ryan met the fireman halfway, standing only a few yards from her. Ryan spoke with the fireman in the street, explaining what had happened, as police officially blocked it off. Then he instructed another county deputy, mentioning Tom the barista—Tori heard that much—who would still be waiting in his sedan in the back alleyway. Two firemen rushed around the alley toward the back of the building, she presumed in search of Tom.

Though Ryan had just been through a traumatic experience or two, he was still the man in charge today and appeared confident and experienced.

And Tori was reminded more strongly than

ever of what she'd lost when she'd left Ryan behind. A lump grew large in her throat. She could hardly swallow.

Ryan suddenly jerked his attention to her, his eyes both searching and piercing, then he jogged around his vehicle to the driver's side. A month ago, Tori would have wanted to be the one in charge. She would never have allowed him to herd her into this vehicle. She would have been very much hands-on in processing this crime scene. But today she'd acquiesced to his demands and was even glad for his over-protective concern.

If he hadn't been there earlier today, she could have been mowed over before she'd even realized she was in danger. She would be in the hospital with injuries. Either that or she'd be in the morgue. Maybe she'd lost her edge.

When Ryan climbed in, she said, "Thank you."

"You're welcome."

She expected him to comment that he was only doing his job. Instead, he started the vehicle and steered out of the cordoned-off block.

"Hey, there's Tom, talking to a deputy. He must be giving his statement." She sighed. "I feel so bad. The café was destroyed because we decided to go there to get warm. Tom was so good to us, and now he's out of a job. We should check in on him later."

"I agree," he said. "We should definitely do that."

He steered onto the main road leading out of Shady Creek and back to Rainey.

Tori suddenly realized she'd used the word "we," and in his reply, Ryan had, as well. Uncertain what that meant, if anything, she turned her attention to watching for anyone suspicious.

"If the place hadn't exploded we could have checked for video footage. I noticed they had a security camera. That could have given us an image of the driver. But we do have the plates now."

"That we do, but I suspect since the driver was so willing to crash it into the café where there would be no retrieving it, they weren't concerned about the license plate tracking back to them."

"You're saying the vehicle was probably stolen."

"Yes."

Both of them caught up in their own thoughts, they drove in silence the rest of the way back to Rainey, where, thankfully, the rain had also stopped, and the sky was clearing.

Who besides Detective Ryan Bradley had followed her all the way out of town to Shady

Creek? Or had they been waiting there for her? The thought gave her the creeps. Maybe she'd been capable of taking care of and protecting herself before, but she was having some serious doubts about her abilities now, in a way that left her feeling vulnerable. She wrapped her arms around herself and wished she had a blanket, even in the warm cab. The weather added to her dreary mood. What happened to the beautiful summer days of northern California? The weather seemed unusual.

She feared that someone might have figured out where she'd been heading and why. Her call to Dee James could have been the catalyst to today's events. She would keep that to herself for now. She didn't want Ryan looking into him and scaring off her only lead.

Still, did Dee James have anything to do with what happened to her today? Had he sent someone to follow her? Or had it been him?

She sat up taller. "You didn't even get a glimpse of the driver?"

"No, why?"

Too bad. If Ryan had said anything about red hair that would have told her something.

"Just wondering."

When Ryan turned onto the street and then parked in front of Sarah's house, Tori realized she'd been so caught up in her thoughts that she'd barely noticed the ride going by.

A deputy waited in a vehicle at the curb. She got out of Ryan's and headed for the house, though she fully expected Ryan would want to clear the house first. She would wait at the door for him. Honestly, she wanted a hot shower and to relax for a few minutes before she had to head over to Mom and Dad's for dinner.

"Tori," Ryan called. He stood next to the vehicle and spoke with the deputy inside.

Tori trudged over.

"Deputy Jackson needs the keys to your car. He'll get it back to you tonight."

Tori nodded and dug through her purse. As her fingers grabbed onto the large key ring that used to belong to Sarah, a pang shot through her heart.

Ryan walked her to the door. "I'm not so sure you should be driving Sarah's car around since we know she was targeted."

"I don't think it matters what car I'm driving. Are you sure you want to use the extra man-power just to bring mine back?" Finding the house key, she thrust it in to unlock the door.

He pressed his hand over hers on the knob. She gazed up at his taller form. She'd once had a thing for him. Might *still* have a thing for him because his nearness seemed to suck the air from her.

"I'll use all the manpower available to me to protect you, Tori."

And she believed him. That thrilled her, when it shouldn't. Warmed her to her toes, despite her cold, damp clothes.

"Now, I'm going in first," he said.

He pulled his weapon as they entered. She disengaged the alarm to allow them entry, then armed it again for protection while they were inside. Like always, Tori waited in the foyer, her own weapon out while he cleared the bungalow again.

Mom texted her.

Dinner ready within hour.

If Mom only knew what Tori had just been through. She would have to keep that from her or else Tori would never hear the end of it.

Ryan returned. "It's all clear, but—" he hesitated "—are you going to be all right? It's been a harrowing day."

She shrugged. "Mom texted that dinner will be ready in an hour. I should be good until then."

His lips flattened into a straight line as if he didn't believe her.

Tori didn't want him to leave yet. Was it only the dangerous situation getting to her? Or was it something more?

"Until then, I'll build you a fire. It'll take the chill off."

She could build her own fire, thank you very much, but if it would keep Ryan here, that was fine by her.

"Still worried about me?" Now why had she asked that? It sounded entirely too much like flirting.

From the way he looked at her, it seemed he'd noticed that, too. A half smile lifted one cheek. "As a detective on this case, yes, I'm worried about you."

His words might have hurt her, if she'd bought into them. With the emotion behind his gaze, she didn't believe his concern was a simple matter of a detective doing his job.

"Okay. I'll just change into clean clothes and then…and then… I'll make us some coffee while you make a fire." That sounded way too romantic, and yet she was walking into this with her eyes wide open.

What are you doing, Tori Peterson?

A few minutes later, as she settled on the sofa with a nice warm fire in front of her and hot coffee in her hand, Tori felt so relaxed that she could fall asleep. She was warm, and with Ryan sitting at the far end of the sofa, she knew she was safe. When was the last time she'd actually felt safe like this? When was the last time she'd allowed herself the *need* to feel safe? It was foolish for her to be here with him now like this, but she needed this.

"You should know that I've been invited to dinner with you and your parents tonight, too." His voice was husky.

The news surprised her. "Oh? Are you going to come?"

"Don't worry," he chuckled. "I have reports to write."

"You sound like you think I wouldn't want you there." Tori sank deeper into the sofa. She was actually considering not showing up, either, but then again, that would hurt Mom and part of the reason she'd stayed in Rainey was for her parents.

"Are you saying that you would?"

She could feel his eyes on her as she stared into the fire he'd made.

Would she? What exactly was she thinking? She edged forward on the sofa and rested her elbows on her knees. "Ryan, believe it or not, I do have regrets about…" *us* "…regrets about everything."

When he didn't respond, she risked a glance at him.

He stared into the fire as if he was afraid to hear what else she might say. The flames flickered softly and the ambience was more than romantic. She should get up. Move around. Ask him to leave. Something.

So she did. Tori moved to stand closer to the fire and rubbed her arms. Maybe she should explain her comment about regrets. "Sarah's death has given me a different perspective on life."

As it well should.

A few seconds ticked by, then Ryan's voice was gentle. "Don't tell me you regret taking the FBI job."

She heard no antagonism or resentment in his tone, which invited her to share her deepest thoughts. "The work has been fulfilling. But now I see that my family should have mattered more to me."

Tears freely leaked from the corners of her eyes.

That you *should have mattered more.*

Suddenly Ryan was there, next to her by the fire. He gently wiped one tear away before turning her to face him. "Your family knows how much you love them, Tori. They're so proud of you. Sarah…she was proud of you."

Why did he have to be so kind and sensitive?

He cupped her jaw and brushed away the tears. Though her mind screamed warning signals, she felt equally compelled to stay right where she was. She ached for his touch, his gentleness. Her heart was like parched, cracked ground and Ryan was a pitcher of cool water.

His lips pressed against hers. She expected a quick kiss of reassurance, but he lingered. Her hands slid over his shoulders and around his neck, pulling him closer. Heart pounding, she soaked in this man. Everything about Ryan that she'd thought she loved at one time.

Oh, how she'd missed him.

He was the one to ease away first, but then he pressed his forehead against hers. She kept her eyes closed while she steadied her heart and held back more tears. Stupid, uncontrollable emotions.

She hated being so vulnerable.

When he released her and stepped away, she opened her eyes. His tortured expression spoke volumes. He was as confused by their kiss as she was.

"I'm so sorry, Ryan," she said. "Kissing you doesn't help. We're trying to work together on this, unofficially, and I don't want to make things more complicated." She should stop talking if all she was going to do was fumble around.

Ryan scraped both hands through his hair, his frustration evident.

Oh. Now she'd hurt him. That hadn't been her intention. Would she ever be anything to him but a huge pain? Surely he didn't want a second chance with her.

"Look, Ryan, not that you're asking me, but I don't deserve a second chance with you." Especially since she wasn't sure that she wanted one.

Far more than the words themselves, Ryan was stung by the tone in her voice, and the complete lack of warmth in her eyes. This was her way of trying to brush him off. He blamed himself for getting in this situation in the first place. He could have put another deputy on the house while Jackson got her car. Ryan didn't have to personally sit in the house with her on the comfy sofa with a fire. And he definitely should never have kissed her—a woman whose sister's murder he was in charge of investigating. He should have never kissed her—the woman who almost destroyed him four years ago.

And he should walk out now, but he couldn't leave without addressing her comment. "Don't worry. I learned my lesson long ago." He grinned, hoping to dial down the tension. If he let it get the best of him, this wouldn't end well.

But he wouldn't let her hurt him again. He would never trust her with his heart. He'd known better than to get his hopes up, which was how he knew he was going to be okay, despite her rejection today.

Regardless, he had to rein this conversation in before it became a full-blown argument. He needed to keep this civil because of what he was about to tell her. So far, he'd kept his distance from her personal investigation into Sarah's murder, but now he needed to shut her down.

First things first. "Your father came by the county offices to see me today."

That brought her chin up. "What did he want?"

"He wants what I want for you. Your safety. That's only going to happen if you stay out of this."

"You told me earlier you knew you couldn't stop me," she said. "And you can't."

"Yeah, well, there was another attempt on your life today, remember? That's two in one day. Someone tried to run you over and when that didn't work, they plowed right into the café! So that changes everything. I can't imagine what Sarah was into that someone is so determined to hide, but so far they've killed four people and now they're going after an FBI agent. This isn't an investigation you can handle as a private citizen. It's just too dangerous."

"They might not know that I'm FBI, Ryan. You give them too much credit when it seems they are becoming careless, which is good for us. We can get the killer sooner."

He took a step closer and tried to skewer her with his eyes. "I'm telling you right now, do not think about continuing to look into her death. Step back from it and hand over everything you've learned so far."

She stepped closer as well and stood taller, unwilling to back down. "Maybe I can never get her back, but I can find her killer. Please don't try to stop me."

"You're exasperating, you know that? Let me do it, Tori. This is my job, not yours."

"Who's stopping you from doing your job? Not me." She thrust her hands on her hips, as if to dare him to stand in her way.

"You've always doubted me. Doubted my abilities. You think you're more qualified to find her killer than I am." His gut twisted as he laid his insecurities out there for her to tromp on.

She raised her arms into the air and moved away to pace behind the sofa. "It has nothing to do with that, Ryan. Nothing at all. I explained this to you. Why do we keep coming back to this?"

"You're right. It does feel like the same old

argument." Like the one they'd had when she left him to move and take a new job. He'd thought he'd gotten over that. But it was painfully obvious to them both that that wound remained and still festered.

Why hadn't he gotten over that hurt? Gotten over her? He must somehow shove aside those forbidden feelings to stay focused on this investigation.

He crossed his arms. "If you're going to do this then I insist you share information with me or I'm going to slap you with obstruction charges."

She narrowed her eyes. "You wouldn't."

"Try me." Ryan set his jaw.

Releasing a slow breath, she said, "I haven't learned anything that could be useful to you, Ryan."

"You were in Shady Creek to follow a lead. That much is obvious. Someone tried to kill you while you were there—to prevent you from finding out more? Don't lie to me."

Her throat moved up and down with her swallow. "Okay. Okay. It's a slim lead, at best. I found out that Sarah participated in an environmental protest in Sacramento with a group called A Better World. Did you know about any of that?" she asked.

"No. My investigation hasn't gotten into the

victims' hobbies or personal causes yet. We've been confirming alibis of all those nearest to the four. Talked to families, significant others, people at their places of employment. I questioned those who worked with Sarah at Gen-Dynamics." Before the attacks on Tori, he was looking into all possibilities for the four victims but looking more closely at Mason's life.

"Her part-time work as an accountant didn't matter to her nearly as much as her volunteering. Sarah was always into social justice and protecting the environment."

"What was the protest about?" Ryan tugged out his pad and pencil.

She arched a brow as if surprised that he was taking this lead seriously, but this could all be important. She obviously thought so, and he wanted to know everything.

"Pollution. I don't know all the details. I think this protest had to do with pesticides used on commercial farms. I haven't spent a lot of time on that. Not yet."

No. She had to go to Shady Creek because she'd found something else. "What triggered you to look into that?"

She scrunched her face. "I've been reading all her emails to me. I never delete emails, so I started as far back as I could find, searching for any hint of activity that might seem suspicious or indicate danger. She doesn't always tell me everything, of course, especially these last few years. I'd been—" she shoved back tears "—My job kept me fully occupied."

Groaning, she rolled her head back and stared at the ceiling and swiped at the tears, clearly frustrated with her emotional state.

His heart kinked. He'd never seen her like this, but then she'd never endured such a tragic loss.

"She mentioned marching in a protest with the environmental group. So I contacted the guy who ran the group. It was clear he knew Sarah, but he didn't offer me answers. Just said he couldn't help me. The conversation had a nuance to it that told me he knew something."

"So you drove out to see him today?"

She nodded. "I had hoped to meet with him, but he'd refused. I figured if I found him and saw him face-to-face, he might be more willing to give me information."

"And what is this guy's name?"

"Dee James."

"Tell me the conversation exactly." Ryan waited with pen ready.

Tori shared as much as she recalled. On the one hand, the guy could be telling the truth about not knowing anything, but Ryan agreed with Tori. There was the hint of something more and it was worth questioning him.

Going there alone to do that had been a dangerous move on her part, but he pushed down his fury at the situation. Beating her up now wouldn't serve any purpose. Still, Ryan couldn't help the admiration that swelled inside at her ability to find a promising lead while he'd only hit dead ends. He simply didn't have enough investigators to dig so deeply. It would take time.

"Good work, Tori."

She hung her head. "Look. I know you don't have the manpower to do this kind of searching. Nor do you have access to communications from Sarah like I do, so please, let me help. I'm sorry… I'm sorry about—"

The kiss.

"It's not your fault, and I'm sorry, too. Let's just forget it ever happened and move on." He was the one to approach her and kiss her, after all. He wouldn't let her carry the blame.

Arms crossed, she shrugged, her right cheek rubbing against her shoulder. The familiar action brought back a flood of memories. "Listen, are you coming to dinner then?" she asked.

"I think I will." It would mean he'd know when she was coming back to the bungalow afterward—that way, he could clear her home again before she settled in for the evening. He would also make sure someone watched her home at all times. "If that's all right with you."

He half expected a frown, but she offered a tenuous grin. "Only if you promise not to say a word to my parents about what happened today. All they need to know is to remain cautious for their own safety because Sarah was a target, which they already know."

"You drive a hard bargain." They might see something on the news channels, but that was in Shady Creek so who knew if it would make the evening news.

Her parents were likely to ask a million questions about the investigation. Maybe eating with them was a bad idea. "Let's make sure to let them know we don't want to talk about the investigation and that it's just a pleasant meal between friends."

Except if they connected just as friends, without the investigation as a distraction, that would mean dredging up the past and too many memories.

EIGHT

Roast beef, potatoes and carrots had been served and eaten. Oh, and homemade rolls, too. Tori's mother had outdone herself, but Tori thought the dinner would never end. She had made it clear that she and Ryan didn't want to discuss the murder investigation.

Besides, she didn't want to scare them or make them worry more than they already were.

So they'd talked about Sarah. Rehashed old but good memories of life growing up. When the conversation had finally waned, Tori yawned.

That had been a perfect segue into announcing it was time to leave. She and Ryan said their good-nights to her parents. This felt far too much like the good ole days when they had dated and grown serious, and her heart was heavy with memories. Add to that, she'd had a hard time shaking thoughts of the earlier kiss she'd shared with Ryan by the fireplace.

At least she had her own vehicle—she'd insisted on driving it to Mom and Dad's rather than riding with Ryan. After they left, Ryan followed her back to Sarah's house in his vehicle. The deputy who had delivered her car remained parked next to the curb. His presence would presumably serve as a deterrent to another break-in or something even more nefarious.

She hoped.

Tori parked in the driveway and waited for Ryan. After parking at the curb he jogged over to her. "Deputy Jackson will stay here and watch your house this evening. He'll be trading off with another deputy close to midnight. I'm not sure whom yet, but I wanted you to know."

At her porch, she nodded. "I truly didn't mean to cause you problems by staying in town. You probably don't need to waste manpower on me, though I appreciate it. I realize that your investigation would be easier without having to worry about me being here."

Ryan said nothing. But he studied her.

Averting her gaze from the handsome detective she might have married, she stared out at the streetlights that barely illuminated the neighborhood and rubbed her arms against the chilly night air. "I know you think it would be easier for you if I went home to South Carolina and maybe even took Mom and Dad with me. But I would be no use to my employer in my current frame of mind. I won't be until this is over. If this is all resolved before my bereavement leave is over, then that's different. I'll be settled and can be of use to my employer." But she had a feeling that she would end up staying no matter what.

"I don't think my investigation would be easier without you," he finally said. "Obviously you've run across information that could help us, but I'm worried about you, Tori. I can't…" His frown lines deepened, then he appeared to rein in his emotions.

What was he going to say? *I can't lose you, too?* She wasn't sure her heart could take this painful dance she and Ryan found themselves in. Bad enough she might not come out of this ordeal unscathed beyond the agony she already suffered at losing Sarah.

"I promise I'll stay alert," she said. "In fact, I'll try to go through Sarah's home again and be more thorough this time. If I can't find anything to help us, then I'll move to a safer location."

"Good. In the meantime, we'll bring Dee James in for questioning."

"No, please," she said. "Let me handle him."

Ryan stiffened.

She'd better reel him in. "If you want me to share information then please let me handle gathering it. I think this guy is spooked. If you bring him in, he'll lawyer up and you won't get a word out of him. But if I approach him alone, he might be willing to talk. I don't think he had anything to do with what happened today."

"How can you be sure?" Ryan asked.

"I can't, but something in his tone on the phone let me know that he cared about my sister. As I've already said, I got the feeling he knows something, but he could be scared and might even run. In fact, he could already have disappeared." She hoped that wasn't the case.

"All right," he said. "I'll give you two days to try to make contact again."

"Come on. You know it could take me that long to hear from him. Give me a week."

He huffed an incredulous laugh. "Are you kidding me? A week is too long. Two days, plus you have to bring me with you if you arrange a meeting. Anything face-to-face and I'm there with you, Tori. It's much too dangerous otherwise. Do you understand?"

She chewed on her lip. Could she agree to that? "Fair enough."

"I'm only agreeing to this because I believe that you're right that he could clam up if I brought him back to the sheriff's offices for questioning."

She saw in his eyes that he hoped she wouldn't make him regret this decision. Tori turned and unlocked the door, disarmed the alarm system. Ryan conducted his usual bungalow clearing and this time, he didn't linger but instead wished her a good evening and left.

She closed the door and locked it, rearmed the system, then peeked out the window. Ryan was talking to the deputy through the vehicle window, his gaze searching the area as he talked. The neighbors had to be wondering what in the world was going on. But that was good. They would be more vigilant about keeping their eyes on the house. That way, they could spot anyone lurking around looking for trouble, out of view of the deputy parked at the curb.

Tori kept all the rooms dimly lit. Nothing harsh and bright, but just enough so there were no dark shadows. She wanted to see every corner. This way she'd prevent any of those too-stupid-to-live moments she often saw in movies when someone crept forward from the shadows.

After the day she'd had, Tori should crash along with the adrenaline in her body, but she wanted to dig back into Sarah's emails. Might as well make a big pot of strong coffee.

She'd contact Dee James tomorrow.

Propped in Sarah's cushiest chair, Tori opened up her emails again and started reading where she'd left off, looking for more about the environmental activities or any other interesting and potentially suspicious mentions.

It was right to stay here and do this. Ryan couldn't investigate this like Tori could. So they would solve this case as a team. And that also felt good and right.

Unfortunately, warm feelings for him flooded her at the thought. She recalled the gentle kiss they'd shared earlier that day and knew without a doubt they both still cared deeply for each other, though neither of them could afford to act on those feelings. Somehow she had to shut down any rekindled emotions that remained for him, which would be hard to do given their current collaboration.

Tori focused back on the emails. She struggled to stay awake, despite the strong coffee. She imagined Sarah's fingers typing the emails, or her smile and eyes as she stared at her laptop. Sarah had been a loving, giving person. The best person that Tori had ever known. The saying that only the good die young seemed true in Sarah's case. Her death was such a huge blow, such a wrongful loss. Tori sniffed to rein in her emotions and the resulting leaky nose.

If Tori was going to help in securing justice for her sister she had to push past the melancholy.

Then she spotted it.

An email sent three weeks ago. In the email, Sarah had added a short line at the bottom about sending Tori a package in the mail. A small intake of breath escaped. She remembered seeing the email now, but just hours after she'd received it, she'd been assigned to a stakeout that lasted for days. Tori—the amazing sister that she'd been—had completely forgotten about the email regarding a package.

Then she'd gotten the shocking news that Sarah had been killed. In a grief-stricken daze, Tori had packed a few belongings and left as quickly as possible. She'd been in a hurry to get to California, so she'd just grabbed the stash of mail she'd yet to go through after her stakeout and crammed it into her briefcase. Whatever didn't fit, she'd put in her luggage to go through later or never.

Tori set her laptop aside and shoved her face into her hands.

I let you down, Sarah!

She shoved from the cushy chair and grabbed her briefcase. She dumped the contents out on the kitchen table and rifled through the envelopes of bills and a few padded mailers, but found nothing at all from Sarah. Next, she moved to the bedroom. She'd hung up her clothes in Sarah's closet next to Sarah's things after the break-in—a pang shot through her—but left the stash of mail in her suitcase.

She dumped the contents of her luggage on the bed and skimmed through more mail—almost all of it junk.

Again she found nothing from Sarah. If Sarah had mailed Tori a package it should be in the stash she brought. She'd left nothing of importance behind in her apartment in South Carolina.

So...whoever had broken into Sarah's home could have found the envelope and taken it. It seemed they had been searching for something, given they had taken nothing else that she could see. The only reason Tori could think that someone would go to that much trouble for the package was because it could contain incriminating information. What Sarah had mailed to Tori could hold the details over which she'd been murdered.

And now, whoever had taken it *could* believe that Tori knew why Sarah had been killed, and it was only a matter of time before she connected the dots to the killer. And only a matter of time before Tori met the same fate as Sarah.

To survive, she would have to beat them at their game before the clock ran out.

The next morning Tori woke up to bright sunshine breaking through the cracks in the mini blinds. Maybe the rain was finally gone and wouldn't return for a while. She stretched and breathed a sigh of relief.

Well, what do you know? I survived the night.

She'd been so exhausted and distraught she was surprised her mind had allowed her to sleep without nightmares, but her body's need for rest had overruled everything else.

Still, her mind remained foggy this morning. If she could have slept another hour or two she would have, but she needed to get busy. Grabbing a cup of coffee from the single-cup coffee maker, she guzzled it before she bothered to get dressed.

She thought about the package she was supposed to have received from Sarah. Was it small or large? What? She didn't know. Sarah hadn't left her any details.

One thing she did know—she'd have to tell Ryan about the package.

She crunched on a breakfast bar and stared at her cell phone. She noticed that she'd received a call during the night but the caller had left no voice mail.

She recognized the number. It belonged to Dee James.

Tori had better fully wake up, and fast. Had she brought trouble to him by going to his address? Did he have any idea that the café's explosion was because someone had tried to kill her? That had all happened right across from his apartment complex. He could know about the explosion but still not know the cause or that she'd been there at all.

Or…he could have been the one to try to kill her. She hoped not. Tori cleared her throat and focused her thoughts, then pressed his number to return the call.

He answered on the first ring. "Hello."

"It's me. Tori Peterson." As if he didn't know the number he'd tried to call.

Per usual he was quiet for a second or two before responding. "I'd given up on you calling me back."

Dee hadn't left a message but obviously assumed that she would recognize his number and eagerly return the call. Maybe he was spooked and didn't want to leave messages.

She responded in kind and made him wait for her reply. Then she said, "You called me in the middle of the night. Sorry, but I just now saw the missed call."

"I'll get right to the point." He responded without waiting. "I've been thinking."

Tori's heart jumped. "So you remembered something that could help me find out who killed Sarah?"

"Yes," he said. "I think we should talk, after all."

"I'm glad you decided to talk, but we're talking right now. What can you tell me?"

"No, I mean…in person."

Okay. "Name the time and place."

"No cops," he said.

"No cops," she repeated and grabbed a pen and a pad. He didn't know she was FBI? Sarah hadn't shared that detail? "Where and when do you want to meet?"

He gave her the address. He was staying at a motel just outside of Shady Creek, toward Redding. She decided she wouldn't mention that she knew where he lived and had been on her way to meet him when she'd been attacked. She suspected she knew why he didn't want to meet at his apartment. He was running and scared. Someone could be after him, too.

"I can be there in two hours," she said.

"I'm not going to wait for you that long. Make it one."

What was with this guy? "Okay. I'll be there."

She ended the call and scrambled to shower and get dressed quickly. Now to get out of here without tipping Ryan off. The guy had said no cops. Ryan had given Tori time to make contact and now that she'd made it, Ryan would also want information out of him. Though Ryan had insisted he needed to come with her to meet Dee James, the guy wasn't going to talk with Ryan there. Tori needed answers.

She peeked out the window. The deputy Ryan had stationed outside her house was still there. Of course. But did that mean that she would be followed when she left the house? Or was the deputy there to watch the property?

Tori got into the car and pulled her cell out in case Dee called. Or in case Ryan called. Dee had sounded scared and had wanted a secret meeting with no investigators—no cops, as he put it. But was this a trap? Did he intend to hurt her?

Even so, she had a weapon and knew how to protect herself.

Backing from the drive, Tori headed down the street, surprised the deputy didn't follow her. He must just be assigned to prevent anyone from entering her home, not necessarily protect or shadow Tori. Good. It wasn't liked she needed a bodyguard.

Tori wouldn't go into this situation if anything raised an alarm or if someone followed her.

A half hour later, she pulled into the parking lot of the Shasta Motel, fifteen minutes early. Good. That would give her time to assess the situation. This time of morning the parking lot was only half full. Either most everyone had checked out, or they hadn't had many guests in the first place. The motel wasn't near any theme parks or anything worthy of entertainment. A family exited their room and climbed into a Suburban. Other than that, the place was quiet.

She drew in a breath.

God, please help me find answers about who killed my sister. You know who it is. Please help me to find the killer and bring them to justice.

Okay, she'd told Ryan she wouldn't do this alone. But as soon as she spoke with Dee and found out what he knew, she would contact Ryan to fill him in. She just wanted to wait until she finally had some answers. Everything she'd discovered so far had only caused her to have more questions. Her weapon hidden beneath her jacket, she headed toward the opposite end of the motel and then made her way down the walkway until she stood in front of the room number Dee James had given her.

She knocked softly. Nothing.

Then she knocked again. "Mr. James? It's Tori."

The door cracked open. She could barely see the redheaded man in the shadows staring out. Hadn't she just last night thought about stupid people walking into the shadows?

"Dee James?" she asked. "I'm Tori. Sarah's sister."

He swung the door wide so she could easily see into the room, for which she was grateful.

She stepped inside and flipped on all the lights to chase away the shadows. "Do you mind leaving that door open while I check the bathroom?"

"Who do you think I have hidden in there?"

She pulled her gun out. He threw up his hands. "Whoa, whoa."

She scrunched her face. "Don't worry, Mr. James. This is for my protection only. I'm checking the bathroom, that's all. I want to make sure this isn't a trap. Is that okay with you?"

He relaxed. "Knock yourself out."

Dee moved to stand in the corner opposite the door he'd left open, which she appreciated. This wasn't the best scenario and she hoped she hadn't just lost his trust.

She glanced at him before clearing the bathroom, then took in the small space in the wall that passed for a closet. He swiped a hand through his hair and fidgeted. Then did it again. Rinse and repeat.

She gestured that he could close the door.

"I don't like guns. Why did you bring a gun? I should have said no guns along with no cops."

"I didn't mean to scare you or upset you. But a girl can't be too careful. My sister was killed. Murdered. I'm only trying to protect myself. That said, I'm going to keep my weapon out and close, if you don't mind." Tori sat in the only chair in an effort to dial down the tension. She hadn't meant to spook him.

"I understand. You don't trust me."

"It's not you." Though she couldn't be sure that he was safe. "I've been attacked a few times since I arrived in California. Now, please tell me what you can about Sarah and what happened to her. It's obvious that you know something."

Sweat beaded his temple to go with his constant fidgeting. Dee began pacing the small room.

"Why don't you have a seat on the bed and calm down?" Tori suggested.

She noted that he acted like someone who was sitting on explosive information and she wanted the information so she could get out of here before things blew up. She would pull pen and paper out, but she didn't want to take the time to write things down. She had a great memory. She had a feeling he wasn't the kind of guy who would allow her to record their conversation.

"Okay. Okay. Sarah…she was always so radical. Outspoken. I think she made some people mad in Sacramento. Some of the legislators."

"You mean when you protested about the pollution issues? Why do you think that *she* made someone mad, specifically? She wasn't the only one protesting."

He shrugged. "She might have threatened someone."

A chill ran over her. "Who did she threaten? How and why?"

"I don't know. Look. I told her to use a secret email. To get an alias, if she was going to be so in everyone's face."

Her sister had used an email to threaten someone. That was what Tori was hearing.

"But isn't that part of the point of belonging to an activist group and protesting? To stir things up and be in-your-face, as you said, in order to affect change?"

"I guess so, yes. I just thought she would take more precautions."

He wasn't giving her enough information to

make heads or tails of this. "When I read up about A Better World, I found a few articles that loosely linked ecoterrorism back to your group. What can you tell me about that? Was Sarah involved in ecoterrorism? Is that what you're telling me—that she threatened politicians with violence?" No way would Tori believe that Sarah would actually hurt someone, but if her targets thought she was dangerous, they might have decided to strike first. Or had Sarah decided to use more subtle tactics to perhaps change laws, like blackmail? There was much more going on here.

Dee's face reddened. "Look. I'm telling you all I know, all right? When I heard about the murders and that Sarah was killed, I wanted to believe that someone hadn't targeted her specifically—that she was just in the wrong place at the wrong time."

"But now you think she *was* targeted. You know something you're not telling me. What did you bring me here to tell me, Mr. James?"

He leaned closer and lowered his voice as if someone could hear them in this room. "She told me that she thought someone had been following her. That she was in danger."

Tori bolted upright then, startling him. "And you're just now telling someone? Why didn't you come forward earlier?" Okay, she was downright angry now.

"I didn't want to get involved—I still don't! I'll deny talking to you or telling you that if questioned. I'm only telling you because you're Tori's sister and I wanted you to know." He stood from the chair and pulled car keys from his pocket. "That's all I wanted to say."

Did he want her to leave or was he the one leaving? Either way, she wasn't done with him yet.

"Why would you deny what you told me to law enforcement? What are you hiding?" Tori put her gun away. It wasn't helping him talk. "Look, I only want to find out who murdered my sister. Are you afraid to admit to some criminal behavior of your own? I already know that Sarah was involved in ecoterrorist activities with you. That's already on the table— you're not helping yourself by keeping quiet about it."

He swiped the sweat from his forehead. "I'm scared. I don't know who I can trust."

"Then come in and let us—" she cleared her throat "—let Detective Bradley and the sheriff's department protect you." Better not to mention her own job title. He probably already knew that the FBI would want him if he was truly involved in ecoterrorism.

"Get real," he said.

"Who did she threaten? I need a name."

"Look, if I knew who Sarah had threatened I would tell you. It happened right after the protest. She got into an argument with a state legislator coming down the steps. A couple of days later, she told me she thought someone was following her. That she'd done something she hoped would make a difference. That's all I know."

"Okay, then, who is the legislator she argued with?"

"Look, there were a lot of people there that day. I only heard about the argument later. I don't know who it was."

Right. Tori wanted Ryan to bring this guy in for questioning. Maybe he could get more out of him. She was running out of patience.

She crossed her arms. This wasn't adding up. This man made it his business to terrify organizations, though he hadn't been caught yet, and now he was running scared? "What's her email alias?"

He shook his head. "I don't know. I told her to use one and that I didn't want to know about it. So she didn't tell me and she didn't communicate with me."

Hmm. "Then what was the point? Who did

she need to email while keeping her identity a secret?"

"I've told you all I know."

Well, that was it. He'd shut down on her. Mr. Dee James was about to meet Detective Ryan Bradley.

"I appreciate you calling me and what you've told me. I wish it was more. If you think of something else, please tell me. I want to get to the bottom of this."

"You should be careful. If what you said is true and someone has attacked you, then you could end up like Sarah. You should stop digging things up and asking questions."

Tori put her hand on the doorknob. That sounded more like a threat. Had Mr. James been playing her?

Gunfire resounded on the other side of the door.

From behind the brick wall where he took cover, Ryan returned fire. He'd already called for backup, but unless they arrived soon, they would be of no help.

He couldn't believe he found himself cornered in the alley next to the motel. He'd followed Tori after the deputy watching the house had contacted him to say she'd left. He'd caught her on the highway leaving town and followed from a good distance so she wouldn't see him. He'd spotted a gunman approaching the motel room and then the man had positioned himself behind a vehicle to shoot her as soon as she exited the room.

Ryan knew he would have to stop the ambush meant to kill Tori. He'd identified himself and tried to detain the man, who then shot at him.

He'd returned fire but had to take cover and now he was pinned behind this wall. This wouldn't help Tori at all, but by now she had to have heard the gunfire. At least she wouldn't be ambushed.

Peering around the wall, he prepared to take another shot. Tori stood opposite him behind a car and fired her weapon at the man.

Ryan reloaded his clip.

"You can come out, Ryan," she called. "He took off."

Ryan stood and cautiously left the cover of the brick wall in time to see that Tori had run after the man and now sprinted down the alley, the rush of adrenaline giving her the boost she'd needed.

Ryan burst from the wall and ran to catch up with her. She paused at the end of the alley.

Gasping, he asked, "What do you think you're doing?"

"I'm going after him." She prepared to peer around the corner.

"Please, let me." He looked both directions. "Clear."

They ran from the alley. "Which way did he go?"

"Not sure. But he couldn't have gotten far. I'll go south, you go north."

"No, we're sticking together." They jogged across the street to a shopping center parking lot.

Ryan stood at Tori's back as they both searched. "We've lost him."

"No, wait." She tugged on his sleeve. "That van is starting up. Can you see who's in it?"

"Not yet. We can watch it drive by." He pulled his cell out to take a picture. Sometimes he wished the sheriff's department had enough funds for the deputies to wear body cams. Maybe next year. That could make his life so much easier. The van passed them.

"I can't tell if it was our guy. The driver was wearing a ball cap. Could have pulled that on as a disguise." Ryan took the photo of the license plate anyway. "We'll run it and see what we come up with."

Tori put her weapon away.

He shook his head and urged her back to the motel until they stood at her vehicle.

"I don't like this. You shouldn't be questioning potential witnesses. You could ruin our case. You know that, right? I was supposed to go with you."

"What case? You wouldn't even have this without me."

"I thought we were working together. You were supposed to call me if you set an appointment with him. It was too dangerous for you to come here by yourself. If I had not followed you then you would have been ambushed. If I hadn't been here, that guy would have shot you the minute you walked out that door."

"Okay, you got me. But I can't say I'm sorry for jumping on the chance to talk to the guy. I appreciate that you saved my life. But Dee called me. He was willing to talk, but he said no cops."

"And we could have kept you safe while you talked to him. You know all this." What had gotten into her except her hazardous need to find Sarah's killer at any cost? "Well, what did you find out?"

She told him everything, including Sarah's email about the package. "But we're here now, and I suggest you question Dee. We don't have time to play games."

Ryan put his gun away for the moment. Together they headed for Dee James's room and knocked on the door.

"Mr. James? It's me again," Tori said. "Detective Bradley would like to speak to you."

They waited but no one answered.

"Mr. James," Ryan said. "You could be in danger. Someone tried to shoot Tori as she exited your room."

A maid pushed a cleaning cart toward the rooms. Ryan was glad she hadn't been in the vicinity of the shots fired. Sirens resounded as other law enforcement showed up.

He flashed his badge and gestured for her to open the door. They didn't have a warrant, but he was concerned that a stray bullet could have hit Mr. James—exigent circumstances. The maid opened the door and they found the room empty.

"He's gone," Tori said. "He must have left as soon as you and I chased after the shooter."

A police officer stepped up to the room. Ryan explained what had happened and contacted Deputy Jackson to bring Dee James in for questioning.

Ryan then walked her back to her vehicle.

Tori lingered at the door but didn't open it. "He said he was scared and didn't know who he could trust. And he definitely won't trust me after this."

"I hope the feeling is mutual and you don't trust him," Ryan said. "That was an ambush."

"So what if it was? It doesn't mean that Dee James arranged it." Despite her words, uncertainty flickered in her gaze.

"We'll get to the bottom of this," he said. "I'm going to follow you home."

Tori made to climb into her vehicle, but he stopped her. "I forgot to thank you for saving me back there."

She shrugged. "You can handle yourself."

"No, really. You had my back. I got cornered. I honestly hadn't expected to see someone gunning for you like that, even after everything that's happened so far." His heart tumbled around. He wanted to pull her to him and hold her—to comfort himself. He pushed aside the ridiculous thought.

"You're welcome, Ryan." She slid into the seat.

"Tori?"

She lifted her gaze to meet his, her green eyes flashing at him. If he understood the timeline, her bereavement leave would run out soon, and then what would she do? Would she really give up her career to stay here? He just couldn't see that happening. If her goal was to be there for her parents then maybe she could somehow transfer to be closer. There was a field office in Sacramento, and resident offices. But he understood agents were often assigned and had few choices.

And why did he care?

"Yes, Ryan?"

"Let's work together. I mean…closely. You can help us with what you know and learn about Sarah, but I can't have you rushing in on your own, ruining our chances of charging someone or getting a conviction."

Subtly nodding, she looked at the ground. "I understand."

Then she started her vehicle. He got into his and followed her back to Rainey. As soon as they pulled into the drive, his cell rang.

Deputy Jackson. He answered.

"Dee James is dead."

NINE

Tori had wanted to go to the scene where Deputy Jackson had found Dee James, but Ryan wouldn't let her. He was letting the techs gather the evidence first, he'd said.

She'd almost been killed. Again. Now she had to wonder if Dee hadn't been the true target. Ryan had assumed the attacker was waiting for her, but what if he'd been waiting for Dee? Or for both of them?

In the meantime, she was back at the bungalow. Another eventful morning to process through, and the day wasn't even over yet. She'd shared with Ryan all the information she'd gathered from Dee, which left her with more questions than answers, and yet, it had sent her in a direction. She would try to find out who the legislator was that Sarah might have threatened.

Getting Sarah's email alias and accessing those emails was critical.

So Tori peered at her own laptop again, but her mind was far from Sarah's emails. She analyzed everything that Dee James had said from their initial phone call through to their meeting at the motel. She tried to think if she'd missed some nuance in his words. Some important information.

Because now he was dead and he couldn't tell them more.

At least, Dee couldn't tell them more in person. But maybe there was something at his apartment, on his cell, or on his computer to help them. Maybe someone else within his environmental activist group knew something to help them. They would need to track down all those involved to question them.

Oh, wait. Ryan had said he would put someone on that. Translation: Tori should stay out of it.

So while she sat in Sarah's comfy chair, on her laptop, Ryan paced in her kitchen. She'd damaged his trust in her when she'd gone to see Dee James alone. Now he was here at the house with her and she wasn't sure he would let her out of his sight again. And she couldn't blame him. He'd refused to leave her side, despite her insistence that she could protect herself. She wanted him out there, working the case, but instead, he was doing his job in her kitchen, speaking on the phone, trying to get a warrant and tech people to retrieve Sarah's digital evidence on top of another possible murder to investigate—Dee James's.

Her heart ached at the thought of his death. The cause of death was a drug overdose, but she and Ryan both believed he'd been forcibly injected—murdered.

She wished she could be officially assigned to work this case. She could almost wish that she worked for Maynor County with Ryan, but even if she did, she would never be assigned her sister's murder case. At least this way, with no official role in the investigation, she had some freedom to look into things in her own way.

Tori concentrated on her conversation with Dee. There had to be something more that he hadn't told her, something that would explain who had killed him—and Sarah. It was all interconnected and Tori focused back on trying to figure out Sarah's alias—she didn't have time to wait on Ryan and his team to get the proper warrants to look through Sarah's computer. Even as her sister, Tori could only give consent to search her own belongings. Anything more could be challenged in court by a defense attorney. Ryan was covering all his bases.

Admittedly she had already been on Sarah's

computer, but now Ryan had a reason to search for digital evidence in his investigation.

Still, Sarah wouldn't have bothered with an alias only to use that on her personal computer. It was like Dee had said—if she was going to email someone with the alias, using her own computer, then there wasn't much use for it.

Who was the person she didn't want to be able to track her down? Whom had she emailed using the alias? And how had they found her?

Ryan approached from behind. "What are you doing?"

"I'm trying to figure out her alias."

"I'm waiting to hear on the warrant for the digital evidence. That includes her alias."

She shoved up from the chair. "You're not going to find anything about the alias on her computer. And we don't have time to wait on warrants. Think about it, Ryan. Someone got to Dee James already. They might already know Sarah's alias address and they could be in the process of erasing the emails. I'm not hurting anything by looking."

He sighed.

"Besides," she said. "Someone keeps trying to kill me. They must think I know more than I actually do. So they want to kill me to keep me from figuring the whole picture out.

They don't seem to understand that attacking me only drives me to try harder."

"All the more reason you need to be somewhere else." He held up his cell. "I've been on the phone to make all the arrangements. I'm moving you to a safe house."

It wasn't a request or even an argument. He'd already made his decision and the arrangements without involving her. He crossed his arms as if he expected a confrontation.

Tori rose to face him, crossing her arms, as well. "I might be a lot of things, but I'm not stupid."

"Meaning?"

"Though staying in Sarah's home has been good for me, and I think it could still help us, I know I should move somewhere they can't find me. That said, I do need to stay here until I can figure out her alias."

Ryan huffed out an incredulous chuckle. "First, you can look for her alias anywhere you can get internet on your computer. Second, what makes you think *you're* going to find it?"

Ryan still didn't get it? "Because I know my sister. She would choose a certain kind of email handle—something with personal significance. That's why, no, I can't just figure it out from anywhere. I have to be here. Just being here in her home, surrounded by her things, her photographs and knickknacks—everything that has Sarah all over it—can trigger that for me."

"But then you'll still have to figure out her password, and how long will that take?"

"Nah. Sarah always used the same one."

Ryan flinched as his eyes widened. "You're kidding."

"Nope. She said she only had so much mental bandwidth, so why try to remember a kazillion passwords." Tori completely understood that thinking, even though she knew it was practically begging a hacker to dive into all of your accounts. "Okay, so you go do your thing. Call someone or something. I need to look through her house and see if I can figure out her email."

The incredulous but amused look Ryan gave her was kind of cute.

Tori started in the kitchen, looking at the placards of nature and verses from the Scriptures. She skimmed through a couple of cookbooks Mom had given Sarah for Christmas.

Lord, please give me some direction.

Hours later, technicians arrived to retrieve Sarah's computer. Apparently Ryan had gotten the warrant to search for digital evidence. Tori had pulled everything from her sister's closet in search of ideas and now she felt ridiculous. Why had she thought this would work?

Ryan approached. "It's time to move, Tori."

"I haven't figured it out yet. I can't leave." He was right about going, and she knew it, but she wanted a few more minutes. Maybe then…

He shrugged. "You might never figure it out."

Tori turned and Ryan was much too close.

"In the meantime, I want you out of danger, Tori." His nearness tugged at her.

Her breath hitched. She wanted to feel his arms around her again. Tori put a hand on his chest and gently shoved him back so she could get by.

"You can still work on it at the safe house," he said. "Sometimes you have to get some distance to get a fresh perspective."

The way he said the words, she wondered if he'd meant something more. If he was talking about their past relationship. And their recent kiss. What would her perspective be on that kiss when she finally got any distance from Ryan? She lifted her eyes to look at him. He studied her. He'd shuttered away the emotions she might have seen earlier. What was he thinking? A better question—did she really want to know?

"All right." She blew out a breath. "I'm going to pack. I don't have much, so it won't take long. But I might need to come back here if I think of something to look into."

He lifted his palms and then dropped them. "If that happens, we'll do what we can. But I think we both know there's nothing here to find or you would have found it already."

"Maybe I can help your computer tech with Sarah's computer."

"We'll see," he said. "Now it's getting late. I want to get you to the safe house before dinnertime."

"What about my parents?"

"I'll inform them that I'm keeping you safe. That's what they want, and they need to trust me for now."

Wow. "But they'll want to see me."

"We'll arrange for that." Ryan's brows knitted. "You know how this works. Why are you wasting time? Let's just get out of here."

Tori couldn't take his intensity and headed toward the bedroom to pack.

She turned to shut the door only to find him standing in the doorway, blocking her.

"Please give me privacy so I can pack," she said.

"I'm sorry. I thought we were still talking." He shrugged. "Thank you for agreeing to this, and also, for what you've learned to help the investigation."

Admiration swam in his eyes. Tori wanted

that from him much more than she should. "You're welcome."

He nodded and stepped back enough for her to close the door. Grumbling to herself, she removed the few clothes she'd put in Sarah's closet and dresser drawers. She was accustomed to living out of her luggage when she traveled, but she'd put her stuff away as if she truly intended to stay here.

Uncertainty about her future gnawed in the back of her mind. Those permanent, life-changing decisions were too big, too important to make while she was in this frame of mind. And yet wasn't it because of the current set of circumstances she was even considering leaving her position?

Tori sighed as she finished packing far too quickly to clear her thoughts. She hadn't brought much. After all, she'd only come out here on bereavement leave. It was only after she'd gotten here that she began to consider extending that indefinitely. She plopped on the edge of the bed and pressed her hands against her face.

Should she go back to work? Ask for a longer extension, or simply resign? She'd need to make that decision over the next couple of days. She wanted to stay close to her parents, but she was in danger, herself, and couldn't be very close to them anyway, since she would be staying at a safe house. Nor could she be as free as she needed to be to conduct her own investigation.

"Oh, Sarah." She lifted her gaze and, through teary eyes, spotted the framed photograph on the dresser. Her sister stood in front of the marina sign in Crescent City with Tori. The picture had been taken before Tori had moved to South Carolina.

The window exploded with shards of glass.

The bedroom door flew open.

"Get out!" Ryan grabbed her and threw her in the hallway as he covered her.

An explosion ripped the air.

His ears rang and dizziness swept over Ryan as he used his body like a human shield to protect Tori. Anguish engulfed him. He should have somehow run farther with her and completely escaped the house before the explosion. But instinctively he'd known there wasn't time and had chosen to cover and protect her.

At least the ceiling hadn't caved in and crushed them.

Shouts resounded and broke through the continuous buzzing in his ears. He needed to get up and get Tori out of here, but his mind and body couldn't agree on how to do that.

Hands gripped Ryan, tearing him from Tori.

His first instinct was to fight the assailant, and he reached for his weapon, prepared to battle and save her.

Deputy Jackson. The breath rushed from Ryan. "I… I could have shot you."

"No, you couldn't. You're moving too slow, Bradley. Are you okay?"

"Yeah. Sure." Ryan glanced down at Tori. Unmoving, she remained on the floor.

Oh, no!

Ryan knelt down next to her and pressed his hand against her carotid artery. She was still alive. Relief whooshed through him.

"Tori." No response. Fear corded his throat. "Tori, are you okay?"

"We called emergency services," Deputy Jackson said. "Looks like it was a pipe bomb someone tossed through the window."

"Is anyone in pursuit?"

"No. I rushed inside to help."

"Did you see who did this?"

Jackson shook his head. "I only heard and saw the explosion."

Ryan wanted to ask Jackson how someone had been able to approach the house and throw a bomb inside with a sheriff department vehicle parked out front. Had Jackson been snoozing or otherwise engaged? Why hadn't he prevented this? But he would save those questions for a better time.

He was worried about Tori.

Tori groaned and rolled over. Her lids fluttered and then opened, and her green eyes focused on him.

He pressed his hand gently against her cheek. "You scared me to death." Had he thrown her to the ground too hard? Maybe she'd hit her head.

"Are you okay?" Her voice sounded weak.

"I'm fine, but you were out for a few seconds."

"No, I wasn't."

"What? Don't you know that you blacked out?"

"Ryan, I was fully aware. I just took my time responding, okay? I feel pommeled by someone's determination to kill me."

Hmm. He wasn't sure he bought that, but then again, Jackson had said Ryan had been moving slowly.

"Okay. Well, good. I'm glad you don't have a concussion. Regardless, an ambulance is on the way." Ryan glanced at the ceiling. "I don't want to move you, but I'm not sure of the house's structural integrity."

She sat up, then pressed her hand against her forehead as if her head hurt. Ryan and Deputy

Jackson reached down to assist her to her feet, but she refused their help.

Ryan took that as a good sign.

Sirens rang out in the distance. But Ryan knew emergency services could sometimes take much too long to arrive. "Let's get out of here," he said.

He, Tori and Deputy Jackson quickly exited Sarah's bungalow. He gripped Tori's arm as he ushered her toward his vehicle.

"I'm okay, you can let me go now." She twisted out of his grip.

"You don't look okay."

At the look of sorrow on her face, Ryan wanted to pull her to him.

She pressed her fingers over her eyes. "Sarah's home is destroyed now."

"Maybe only her bedroom—it's too early to say. But it can be repaired, Tori. The house is just a thing. It's not a life."

"Her bedroom is the most important room. There were photo albums. Things I still needed to go through. And what about my things?"

He frowned. "We don't know about the damage yet. We'll have to wait and see. At least you left your laptop on the coffee table." But he knew her suffering had less to do with the material things than with the emotional weight of losing another piece of her sister.

"Come here." He wrapped his arms around her. He should be more concerned about her and less about protecting his own heart and keeping his distance.

He held her a few moments, then urged her to sit in his vehicle until the ambulance arrived. Ryan turned to his deputy, who stood waiting with him. "Have our techs check the house for cameras and bugs of any kind."

When he focused back on Tori, her eyes were wide and clear.

Good. Maybe she really hadn't blacked out. "Next time, we might not be this fortunate."

"Someone knew I was in my room and threw the bomb through the window. They knew I was there."

"Exactly what I was thinking. It could have been a coincidence that you were in the room when the bomb came through, but you know I don't believe in those."

"That means either they were watching me through the window—" she glanced across the street "—or the initial break-in could have included someone installing a camera or listening devices. The creeps." She shuddered.

"They could be searching for the information Sarah had, and hoped you would find it. That would be a reason to watch you."

She scrunched up her face. "That makes no

sense. If they want me to find something for them, why try to kill me?"

"It could be both. They want you dead, but they also want to know if and when you learn something. In this case, they might have heard our discussion of moving you and decided to try to take you out before it was too late."

A chill crawled over Ryan and he hovered near her to protect her. "You should wear a vest at all times now."

"What makes you think I don't?" She lifted her sleeve enough for him to see a light body armor.

Any other time and he would have chuckled. He'd hugged her, so he knew that she had one on now. The body armor served as a reminder that if he had gotten her out of the house and somewhere safe sooner, Sarah's house would likely still be intact, and Tori wouldn't have almost lost her life again.

If he hadn't lingered in the hallway, he wouldn't have been there to yank her out. Would she have reacted differently and died in the explosion?

A fire truck finally arrived, as well as an ambulance for Tori. Ryan allowed a paramedic to check him out but refused the full exam at the hospital. He insisted that Tori go, and then from there, they would head to the safe house.

His biggest fear at the moment was her safety on the way to the hospital and while she remained there. Whoever was behind these attacks was determined, and they had stayed ten steps ahead of his investigation.

A familiar vehicle steered up to the curb. Oh, no. Tori's parents. They couldn't have come at a worse time. Had they heard the sirens or maybe been on their way home and followed emergency vehicles here? Or maybe they just wanted to check on their only living daughter.

David Peterson jogged around his vehicle as Sheryl got out, and together they crossed the street. Both their faces were pale and somber. David kept a protective arm around Sheryl.

The ambulance drove away with Tori.

"Ryan?" David asked. "What's happened here? Where's Tori?"

"She's in the ambulance, but she's fine."

Tori's mother started sobbing. "She's not fine if she's in an ambulance. What's going on?"

"I assure you, she's okay. She got knocked to the ground, so a doctor should take a look at her, but mostly I wanted her out of here. I'm going to meet the ambulance at the hospital." He wanted to reassure them, but he wouldn't lie or pretend that Tori wasn't in significant danger.

"You didn't answer my question. What happened?" David asked.

"An explosion of some kind. Listen, you two, we have everything under control, but you should know I'm moving Tori to a safe house."

David's mouth dropped open. "What?"

"You wanted me to keep her safe, remember?"

"And now that you've failed again, you're finally doing something?" Anger had replaced Sheryl's whimpers.

He wanted to reply that their daughter was nothing if not stubborn, and very capable—he couldn't protect her if she insisted on running directly into danger. But arguing with her parents over whether or not he was at fault wouldn't do any of them any good. "I'll call you later."

He climbed into his vehicle.

"We're coming to the hospital, too," David said.

Ryan groaned inside. His biggest concern at the moment was Tori's safety, and if her parents were there then he only saw them getting in the way. Their interference wouldn't help. But their daughter had come by her stubbornness naturally—he could tell they wouldn't back down, so he didn't bother trying to convince them.

He radioed for law enforcement to meet the ambulance and a deputy to remain with Tori at all times until he got there. His job as an investigative detective had suddenly morphed into him doubling as a bodyguard.

TEN

Tori was getting tired of seeing the inside of a hospital, especially since her parents and Ryan were having a confab in the hallway without her. Unfortunately, the doctor had insisted he keep her for overnight observation. She hadn't convinced Ryan that she hadn't been knocked unconscious. She couldn't be 100 percent sure herself. And her shoulder was giving her fits.

But morning was here. She'd stayed overnight and she was ready to go. She found new clothes her mother had bought for her and put them on. Jeans and a T-shirt and a zippered hoodie. Perfect.

Ryan was much too focused on Tori's safety, for which she knew she was partially to blame. She hadn't done such a great job convincing him she could protect herself. But it was like he'd told her—under normal circumstances she *could* protect herself, but being targeted was far from normal.

Sarah had thought someone was following her—and in that way, she'd even done a better job of staying alert to danger than Tori had. Had she experienced any other kind of threat to her life that they hadn't uncovered?

Tori squeezed her eyes shut. *God, please help us to find who did this to Sarah. Please... Help me. Show me the way.*

The door opened, startling Tori from her prayer. The nurse handed over the paperwork for Tori to sign, which she quickly did and met her family in the hallway.

She took in their expressions. Uh-oh.

Ryan's face had grown even more somber. Mom's face was paler than she'd ever seen, and Dad's was red and twisted with anger.

How she wished they could have been spared.

Tears formed in Mom's eyes and she hugged Tori to her and sobbed. At this moment, Tori wished she was two thousand miles away. She'd only brought them more heartache by being here.

"I'm so sorry, Mom. I didn't mean to put you through this on the heels of..." She couldn't say Sarah's name when referencing her death. Not to her parents. It hurt too much. "I only meant to help."

Mom released her, then Dad stared down at her, his expression stern, as if she were still a child. "I insist you go home to South Carolina now. Go back to your job and leave the investigation to the authorities."

Tori frowned and fought the need to defend her decisions. She wasn't a child, even if her father insisted on treating her like one. "I can't have this discussion with you. Not here. Not now." Maybe not ever.

Turning her back on them, she walked away, hating herself for the seemingly heartless action. It was anything but heartless—too many emotions were getting in the way of her talking to them, causing an abyss to expand between them.

She stopped at the elevator, hoping for an escape. She had considered remaining in Rainey even after the investigation concluded because she believed her parents needed her. They all needed each other after Sarah's death. But now she wasn't sure she could tolerate her father's attitude. Would he always be this overprotective, this controlling if she stayed? She couldn't be sure—and she knew it wasn't fair to judge him based on his behavior right now, when emotions were running far too high. They all needed a little bit of grace and mercy for each other right now.

Footsteps approached from behind. She knew that cadence.

Ryan.

Unbidden, her heart danced around inside. She shoved those nonsensical feelings away, or rather, tried to.

He sidled up next to her. "So you're just going to leave them like that?"

Tori pressed the elevator button, then angled her head toward him. "It's an argument that can go nowhere and might escalate into something truly hurtful. I'll call them later. They'll get over it. You should know how it works in families. You have a bigger one than I do."

He hung his head and shrugged, then lifted his chin, his eyes pinning her. "He loves you, that's all. He's worried about you."

And so are you.

"I know. You feel the same way he does. You want me gone."

Ryan said nothing in response as the elevator door finally dinged and then opened.

Together they stepped into an empty elevator, but not before Tori noticed her parents chatting with the doctor, Rick Hensley, whom her dad knew. Good, they were distracted. A pang shot through her heart.

The elevator doors closed them in. "I'm at the end of my rope, Ryan. That's all. Now please take me somewhere safe so I can get

busy again. If my laptop and purse can be re-
covered, I'm going to need those, too."

"We're going to find him, Tori, I promise."

"Don't you think you're a bit overconfident?
You can't make that promise." The words came
out sounding harsh, which she hadn't intended.

She caught a bit of her contorted reflection
in the small mirror in the corner. She was a
wreck. Tori combed her fingers through her
hair so she could look more presentable.

Ryan said nothing at all, but in the reflection
she saw his lips had flatlined.

"Look, I'm sorry," she said. "Your retort
should have been, 'And you're the one who's
going to bring him down?'"

He chuckled.

Good. She liked the sound of it. That was
exactly what they needed more of around here.
She allowed herself to laugh, too.

"I can't say I wasn't thinking it," Ryan said,
"but it's been a rough day and tensions are high.
I don't need to add anything inflammatory."

She shifted to face him. These elevators
could take an eternity. "I'm glad we've at least
come to the place where we can laugh about our
ridiculous…competition, I suppose—though
that doesn't seem like the right word."

"We're not competing," he said. "We're
working together. I'm working closely with

you, the person who knew Sarah the best, to find the answers, so my team and I can build a case and get this guy behind bars. But in less than a couple of days, you'll have to return to work because your bereavement leave will be over. And I know you, Tori. You'll go back."

The way he grinned with his words, he was simply letting her know what he knew to be true, even if she didn't feel she knew it herself yet.

She lightly punched his arm. Tori hadn't officially left the feds, though it had been in her heart and mind. But she didn't want to make such a drastic decision when she was grieving.

Finally the elevator doors opened.

"Tori." He held her back. "Let me go first. We'll meet a plainclothed deputy in the lobby and get into that vehicle. We'll change to another vehicle a few miles down the road, just to be sure."

His words took her aback. "Wow," she said. "I'm impressed."

"Believe it or not, impressing you wasn't my goal."

Oh, he was being funny again. She walked with him to join a deputy she hadn't met yet and the three of them climbed into an unmarked SUV. Someone could follow them from the hospital, so the deputy drove around town for fifteen minutes until they were certain no one had followed, then they turned into a parking garage at the local bank building, where Tori changed into a wig and cap. Ryan simply wore a hat and different sunglasses for his disguise.

"You've thought of everything." She climbed into the new vehicle.

From the driver's seat, he glanced at her, dimples carving into his cheeks. "Were you expecting anything less?"

She couldn't help smiling at him—gone was the animosity between them. He'd resented her for the longest time, believing she thought she was better than him because she was a federal agent. But while she'd wanted something different from the Maynor County Sheriff's Department, she admired Ryan and his abilities. "No, Ryan. I wasn't."

That brought a satisfied grin to his face.

The easy camaraderie between them made it that much harder for her to keep to herself what she'd learned moments before the pipe bomb had been tossed through the bedroom window.

Ryan finally steered the vehicle up the winding drive to the home loaned to him by Jasper Simmons, who was away on vacation. Ryan had saved Jasper's son from drowning when the boy had fallen into the Wind River and then been whisked away by the swift current during a fishing trip. Ryan, who had been on the river in a boat at the time, had been able to reach the ten-year-old boy before he went over the falls. Afterward, Jasper had told Ryan to call him if he ever needed anything, anytime. Day or night. Ryan had made that call and now Tori had a house in which she could be safe for the time being.

Tori sat up taller as the long drive continued to wind around and Mount Shasta came into view. White patches could still be seen on the peak in the summer—glaciers remained at the highest points and never melted. Up close and personal, the mountain was breathtaking.

"Would you look at this view." She moved the visor so she could see better out the window. "Okay, now I really do think you're trying to impress me."

He parked the vehicle in front of the sprawling log cabin. "Now why would I want to do that?"

Tori said nothing to his question. It was only light banter, so she shouldn't be offended. Impressing Tori hadn't been his intention. All he'd wanted to do was to keep her safe.

Hopping out, he jogged around to open the door for her, but she had already climbed out.

Hands on her hips, she stared at the mountain as though she hadn't grown up in the shadow of Mount Shasta. Still, unless you hiked to the summit or lived in a place like this, this view wasn't something you saw every day.

"The Karuk tribe call it White Mountain," she said. "Did you know that it's the second highest peak in the whole Cascade range?" She turned to look at him and laughed.

"I didn't realize you were so fascinated with it," he replied.

"So there are still a few things you don't know about me. I'm glad I can still surprise you."

She was glad about that? He tried not to consider the implications.

"And now, I have a surprise for *you*." He smiled.

"Oh, yeah? What's that?"

He opened the back of the vehicle. "Your stuff's in the back."

Tori pressed a hand to her forehead. "I'm so relieved, Ryan. Thank you!"

She strode over to the back of the vehicle to stand next to him.

He handed off her laptop, a duffel bag of newly purchased clothes—since her others had been destroyed—and her purse that seemed to survive everything. "We've taken the liberty of going through your belongings in search of listening, visual or tracking devices."

"Of course. I'm glad you did." She shouldered her purse and held the laptop under her arm.

When she reached for her duffel bag, he snatched it. "I've got this."

"Thanks." She waited for him to shut the back. "Well, are you going to give me the grand tour of this place?"

"You and I will get the grand tour together. I don't know my way around, either. We'll have to go exploring. I hear it has two ponds and a creek. But, of course, I'll need to make sure the area is safe. No going off the property. Understood?"

"Understood."

Together they hiked to the porch, up the steps and to the door. Ryan fumbled around in his pocket and found a key. Jasper's mother kept a spare and Jasper had instructed her to hand it off to Ryan for the time being.

Inside the home, Tori set her things on the floor, her gaze traveling up and over the log walls and ceiling. The home featured a large open kitchen with soapstone counters and stainless steel appliances.

In the living area they found custom wood-carved furniture to go with the cabin. Tori sighed. "Okay, now this is my dream home. I never had a dream home before. Sarah wanted a house like the bungalow she got."

No, you didn't have a dream house—just a dream job...

Crossing her arms, Tori strolled through to the great room, where she stood in front of the panoramic window with a view of Mount Shasta. "Yeah. Dream house."

Ryan moved to stand next to her and take in the view.

"Just breathtaking," she said, then eyed him. "Okay, Ryan. You've ruined me. I didn't know I was missing anything until you brought me to this house."

Tori smiled. Her golden hair and green eyes with that mountain in the background... Um... Yeah... Breathtaking. The mountain alone couldn't do that for him. A knot lodged in his throat.

Why had he let this woman get away from him? In his heart, he'd known that she had to leave and take the opportunity presented to her, but it made his heart ache to think of how he had let her go and not tried to persuade her to stay. She'd never even asked him to come with her, so he hadn't presumed she wanted him to.

There was the old adage—*If you love something, let it go. If it comes back to you, it's yours forever. If it doesn't, then it was never yours at all.*

Tori obviously hadn't been his to begin with.

She'd had to make her dreams come true. So he'd been right to simply let her go, even if he'd been crushed and then allowed anger and resentment to take root.

But he was done with that, he hoped. He was glad that she'd achieved so much. Not many people had the strength to go after their dreams with such single-minded determination.

Ryan didn't trust himself to speak, so he kept quiet.

Tori angled to look at him and offered a soft smile that did uncontrollable things to his heart.

"All I know is that I'd better not get used to this place because I'm not going to be here that long and it might be painful to leave if I get too attached."

He chuckled. "Sometimes you can't help getting attached."

No matter the effort put in to stay disentangled. Her eyes flashed with emotions, and he sensed that she'd understood his deeper meaning. See, he shouldn't have trusted himself to speak.

Her expression turned serious. "You're going to find the person responsible for Sarah's death and the attacks on me just like you've reassured me repeatedly."

She was obviously trying to redirect him. Refocus him back on task. No pressure there. He found himself searching for the right response when the doorbell chimed. Perfect timing.

"Ah, that must be your protective services," Ryan said.

Tori's eyes narrowed. "I thought *you* were my protective services."

Was she disappointed? He had the strong feeling that she was, and that was too much to process. He had the sudden urge to kiss her, which just told him he needed to step away. "I have to investigate, remember? And find this guy, just like I *reassured* you."

Emotion swirled in Tori's eyes and she appeared speechless, which might be a first. Wow. Entirely too much chemistry brewed between them. Was it because they had nearly lost their lives multiple times? Traumatic events had a way of pushing people together, making them closer under pressure.

He opened the door to let in a female deputy who would stay with Tori. Admittedly, he'd brought Deputy Shawna Reiser into this to free himself up not only to investigate, but to put distance between himself and Tori. And now part of him wished he hadn't, but that was only because his emotions were getting in the way, which should never happen. Tori had to know that his heart was getting involved when it shouldn't, and as much as he wanted to protect her personally, it was more important that he solve the murders. An emotional involvement on his part would jeopardize the investigation.

Now he was glad he'd made the decision ahead of time. He found Tori in the kitchen eyeing the bananas. "I thought you said they were on vacation. Why are there fresh bananas on the counter?"

"Jasper's mom knew we were coming and stocked a few items." Ryan hadn't liked that even one more person knew about their current location but it couldn't be helped. "I'm heading out. Remember to let me know if you learn anything new."

She peeled a banana. "I'd appreciate the same consideration. That will help both our efforts."

"Will do." He left her in the kitchen and headed for the front door. Shawna stood there, waiting. "Don't forget to lock up. Check all the windows and doors and keep an eye out. I don't expect any trouble, but this guy is determined and we can't be too careful."

He opened the door to step outside.

"Detective Bradley," Shawna spoke in low tones. "Ryan…"

Shawna and Ryan had some history—a short time of seeing each other before they'd realized that they would make good friends but nothing more. She'd been hurt in the past, as had Ryan, and neither of them had been truly ready to move on.

Hesitating, he shut the door. "Is there a problem?"

"Yes. This house is far too big to adequately protect someone, don't you think? And the windows? She's far too exposed here. Whose idea was this?"

"I understand your concern," he said. "But it was the only house available and you have to admit that it's far off the beaten path. She won't be easy to locate. This will give us some breathing room since we know she can't stay in Sarah's home or with her parents. Besides, if someone actually finds her, it's not going to matter how many windows there are."

He opened the door again, though he had more to say. "Don't worry, I'll check in on her. But I don't want a lot of people going back and forth here. Other than Jasper and his mother, only you, me and my captain know that we're using this location. Let me know about anything suspicious. Anything at all."

Frowning, she nodded, clearly not happy with the location. "I'll do my best, Detective."

"That's all any of us can do," he said and turned again to leave.

"Ryan…" she shifted to a more personal tone "…it's her, isn't it? This is the woman you hadn't gotten over yet back when you and I dated."

He subtly nodded. He was afraid to ask her what gave him away. Not wanting to get any further into that conversation, he took another step out the door, officially shutting any more questions down. "I'll check the perimeter before I leave."

With that, Ryan finally closed the door behind him. He got a pair of binoculars out of his vehicle and then hiked around the house. The log cabin was positioned on a ridge on the north side, so at least they didn't have to worry about an intruder from that direction. No one was going to climb the ridge to enter the house. Still, he peered through the binoculars in all directions and saw nothing but nature and wildlife for miles around.

Satisfied they were utterly alone out here, he marched back to his vehicle and made to open the door.

"Ryan!" Tori called as she jogged over.

"Something's wrong already?" He left the door open but didn't get inside.

"No." She shook her head, then said, "I mean, yes."

He crossed his arms and waited.

"Right before the explosion in the bedroom, I found something. Remember I mentioned looking for a trigger?"

"I remember."

"I found a picture of Sarah and me together in Crescent City. She'd wanted to spend time with me on the coast before I moved."

"And that's the trigger?"

She nodded vehemently. "I thought it could be her alias."

"And you're just now bringing this up to me, why?" He dropped his arms and fisted his hands.

Tori blinked. "I couldn't know for sure."

His heart rate jacked up. "And now you do."

"Yes." Her right cheek hitched up with her half grin. "I found her alias, and I think you should stay."

ELEVEN

Tori couldn't read Ryan's expression. She had hoped he would be as excited by this breakthrough as she was. Was he disappointed in her for not telling him right away?

"Look, an explosion got in the way of me telling you right when I noticed the picture. Okay? That and, well, I wanted to make sure. Why waste your time if it was a dead end? You understand, don't you?" Why was it so important to her that he did?

He shut the door and locked up his vehicle, then walked with her back to the house. "It's not important now. But next time, please share anything with me right away, whether you think it has merit or not."

Shawna held the door for them, and Tori led Ryan through the house to the spacious breakfast room, which had a view as amazing as the one from the great room. Her laptop sat open on the table.

At the stern expression remaining on Ryan's face, Tori tried to lighten his mood. "If only I could have this view every day while I have my morning coffee." Ugh. She really had to come up with something better to say than going on about the log cabin.

He shifted a bit to look her full in the face, and then offered a weak grin. "I couldn't agree more."

His words pushed into her and through her, along with certainty that he wasn't talking about the view through the window. Her pulse kicked up. *This isn't happening. This can't happen between us.*

Tori forced her eyes to her laptop while she calmed her heart. She pulled out a chair at the table to sit in front of the computer so she could show him what she'd found. But Ryan remained standing.

"Well, are you going to sit down?" she asked.

"I'm fine here, thank you."

And she had the distinct impression he was working hard to keep space between them. She understood completely.

She awakened the laptop and showed Ryan the webmail screen. "She used the server she was familiar with, only she probably always logged in from a public computer when she was using this email. Like I said, she always used the same password. And if she was using an alias that no one should associate with her, why come up with a new password?"

"I think it would have been better to give the tech guy the alias, Tori. You're stepping onto shaky ground here since we have the warrant for digital evidence. We want things processed correctly."

"You said you wanted my help."

"I do."

She could feel his warmth, his breath against her face as he leaned close to peer at the screen.

"Do you want to look at her emails or not?" Her voice sounded too tremulous.

"Let's see them." Ryan's voice, however, was firm and confident.

Still, she sensed that her nearness affected him the same way his impacted her. Time to focus on the task. She blew out a breath.

Together, they opened and read several emails.

"I can't believe this," Tori said. "It sounds like she was digging around in the environmental group. Like she was involved as an activist to find out about their ecoterrorism activities." Tori let out a sigh. "Honestly, that sounds more like Sarah. I can't believe she would ever be involved in illegal activities even for a cause she believed in, or threaten anyone, like Dee James suggested."

Ryan finally pulled up a chair to sit next to Tori. "I don't understand why Dee told you he was the one to suggest she use an alias for an email, since she was looking into *his* group and activities. But it looks like he told the truth when he said she never contacted him from this account. She *was* emailing someone else, though. We need to know who this person is."

"He also said she thought someone was following her," Tori said. "Could it have been someone with the environmental group? Except that doesn't make sense—Dee was scared himself. Obviously for good reason because someone killed him." Maybe Dee had turned against the more violent extremists in the group after they killed Sarah? Maybe that was why he was willing to talk to Tori—and why he was killed?

She scratched her head, wishing she could figure this out.

"Right. There's that, but let's focus on these emails. Who is she talking to here?"

"Ned Hundley. We can't know if that's also an alias, though," Tori said. "Wait a minute."

She turned to look at Ryan, realization reflecting in his gaze.

"She was an informant," they said simultaneously.

Tori shoved from the table.

"And who investigates ecoterrorist groups?" Ryan asked, though he already knew.

"The FBI." Fury boiled through her veins. "I can't believe this!"

She rushed from the breakfast room to the living area with the panoramic view of Mount Shasta and then finally settled to stare out the window.

Ryan approached from behind, then stood next to her. "You think both of them should have told you."

"Whatever my employer did or didn't do, whatever the Bureau's involvement, I think *she* should have told me." Grief and anger twisted inside.

What was the purpose in working for the FBI if she couldn't keep her own family safe? How had Sarah ended up working with the FBI as an informant? Had she been caught for being involved in something illegal and then forced into becoming an informant to clear her own record? That was how it often went down. Nausea swirled in Tori's gut and she pressed her hands against her midsection.

Knowing her sister, Tori felt it was more likely they somehow convinced Sarah that she was going to help them to prevent something terrible from happening. That would be very in character for Sarah. The queasiness eased up a bit.

Still next to her, Ryan sighed. "Maybe she was approached and then once she agreed, she was instructed not to share the information with anyone. Not even you."

"I need to contact this Ned Hundley. If that's even his name," Tori said.

Ryan started pacing along the large, panoramic window. "This has shifted into a new investigation. If she was killed because of her informant status, the FBI should be investigating her death. They would also be investigating Dee James if he's tied into this, too. So why aren't they?"

Tori pulled out her cell. "I'm going to find out."

Ryan urged her hand down. "You're on bereavement leave, remember? You're not supposed to be working a case. Let me reach out. In fact, I need to send what we've learned over to computer forensics techs working on Sarah's digital evidence. Maybe they can also find out more about Ned Hundley, if that is his real name. Let's work this through the proper channels so we can build our case."

Reluctantly she put her cell away. He was right. She turned to face him and looked into his intense blue-green gaze. She'd been such an idiot to leave him behind to pursue her dream job. The FBI might have resources that took her work to a higher level…but the Maynor County Sheriff's Department had a degree of trust and respect among colleagues that the Bureau was clearly lacking, especially since it looked like someone within the ranks of that organization had used her sister and gotten her killed. The bitter truth of it stung.

Tori didn't know how to process the information. She wished she was back at work and in her office now so she could face off with someone as anger boiled through her. On the other hand, it was better that she was here now and with Ryan.

"I'm glad you're in this with me." She couldn't believe she'd admitted that to him. Now the fact that she'd said his name after she'd been pulled from the falls made so much more sense. But deep inside, she also knew that her need for him in this investigation went much deeper than the simple fact that he was the investigating detective.

She hung her head and hugged herself.

"Tori…" The way he said her name curled around her heart.

He pulled her into his arms and Tori soaked up the strength of Ryan's broad shoulders and sturdy chest, when she shouldn't. She savored the comfort that poured from his heart, when she shouldn't. She had no right to take from him when she had nothing to offer in return.

But she needed to feel his arms around her, if only for a moment.

"Detective—"

Deputy Reiser abruptly entered the living room, startling them both, and Ryan suddenly stepped back. He hadn't meant for the deputy to see him holding Tori.

Shawna cleared her throat.

"What is it?" Ryan's tone was sharp with frustration.

"I think someone is lurking in the woods."

His shoulders stiffened. "Tori, get away from the window."

He pushed a button that lowered the enormous shades. Shawna's earlier words about the size of the home and the windows came back to him. He hoped she was wrong about a lurker.

"Show me," he said to Shawna.

She rushed around the house and through the kitchen to look through the window in the breakfast room. Tori tried to follow Ryan and the deputy, but he turned and gently grabbed her arm. "I want you to stay in a room without windows for now. Please."

Tori nodded and fetched her laptop from the table and then disappeared down the hall.

Shawna studied the woods. "Whoever it was is gone. I don't see him now."

"It was a 'him'?"

"Yes. I think it was a male but from this distance I can't be positive."

Ryan scraped a hand down his face. "Are you sure he was lurking? As in, watching this house?"

She shrugged. "What else would you call it when someone gets that close to a house on private property and seems to be hiding in the trees? You said to tell you if I saw anything."

"I'm glad you did, but I need all the facts, Shawna. Are you sure he was on the property? Not just in the public woods?"

"I haven't actually gone out there to mark off the property line." Shawna was growing irritated at his questions. "But even if he wasn't on the property, if he was standing behind a tree to watch the house, that's something to note."

"You're right."

But he couldn't fathom that someone had found Tori yet. He didn't want it to be true.

Ryan retrieved his weapon from his holster. "After I leave, lock the door. If you haven't already checked all doors and windows, please do so now, and then stay with Tori and keep her out of sight. Remain aware and on the lookout for someone outside trying get in. I'll communicate with my radio."

"But what about you?" Shawna asked. "Do you want me to call for backup?"

"I'll check it out first. It could be nothing. If you hear gunfire, then you can call."

Weapon ready, he made his way to the back of the house in search of an exit. Then he carefully slipped out through a door in the mudroom. The surrounding woods were vast, offering way too many opportunities of places to hide.

He waited and listened to the sound of wildlife—insects and birds. A squirrel jumped from a tree branch. A golden eagle screeched in the sky. If someone was close, they could disrupt those sounds, but the natural world gave him no hint of a man's presence. Ryan calmed his breathing.

If someone had come for Tori, that meant this safe house was no longer safe.

Please let Shawna be wrong about this.

But despite his wishes, he knew that Shawna was no fool. Keeping to the shadows, he crept to the other side of the house, his eyes searching for movement in the woods. These woods were thick with evergreens—red-and-white fir, Douglas fir, a variety of pines. Mountain mahogany and junipers also thrived. Underbrush was thick here, as well, and would make getting to the house difficult.

It could also make tracking someone easier. If someone was in those woods, he had to find them. It didn't matter that he didn't want to leave Tori behind.

Holding his gun at low ready, he left the house behind him and entered the forest of evergreens, watching the pine needles and underbrush for signs of humanity. After half an hour of traipsing through the woods, he found no evidence that someone had been lurking.

In the nearby distance, a vehicle roared to life. Ryan took off running through the woods, jumping over underbrush where necessary, dashing around trees and pushing his way through underlings. He ran toward the sound until he made it to the river.

Gasping for breath, he watched a Jeep utility vehicle driving away on a dirt path. He wished he had his binoculars so he could catch the license plate, but he had left them in the house. Still, he made note of the make and model, and the kayak sticking out the back.

Ryan hiked his way back to the house, palming his pistol. How could he know if someone had simply taken that path to kayak the river, or if someone had intentionally crossed the river to try to get closer to Tori? And if they had made their way to the house deliberately, then how had they found out where she was staying so quickly?

By the time he made it back to the house he was frustrated and breathing hard. Ryan spotted a vehicle through the trees exiting on the long drive. Panic spiked through him. He sprinted to the door and tried the knob. Fortunately, it remained locked. He rang the doorbell.

Shawna let him in. "Did you see him?"

"No. But I spotted someone exiting the drive. Did anyone come to the house while I was gone?"

She shook her head.

Despite her reply, Ryan knew one thing. "That's it. This house is obviously compromised. I can't be sure that Tori will be safe here. Would you mind helping her get her things? I'll take her somewhere else."

"But where?"

"I'm the only one who will know this time."

"I promise you, I told no one," she said.

"I know I can trust you," he reassured her. "There are at least three other people who know we're using this house for a safe house, and there are many other ways to find out."

He was most worried about those other ways.

TWELVE

Tori couldn't believe that she was standing in the living room of Ryan's home.

"Your house? Really, Ryan? What are you thinking? I might as well move back to Sarah's bungalow since it's only a few houses down." That is, as soon as the crime scene was released and construction work made the place livable again. Oh, she couldn't believe any of this.

"It's temporary, okay?" Ryan scraped a hand down his face. An action she'd noticed him doing an awful lot of lately.

"Okay." She tried to soften her earlier incredulity.

"It's just until I can figure something else out. And don't worry about—"

A door opened and shut somewhere in the house, interrupting what he might have said. Ryan palmed his weapon, and Tori grabbed her own. Had whoever found her at the big dream house followed them here?

"Hi, honey, I'm home," a lilting female voice proclaimed.

Jealousy snapped through her. Ryan… He had someone? Who was—

Ryan's twin sister, Katelyn Bradley, strolled into the room with a large reusable grocery sack that she set on the counter with a thunk.

Tori relaxed and put her gun away.

"You nearly gave me a heart attack." Ryan returned his weapon to the holster at his waist. "I forgot you were coming over."

"See," Katelyn said. "This is why we never get together. You forget about me. I'm your twin. How could you possibly forget?"

"It's been one of those days, okay?" He winked at his sister. To Tori, he said, "I texted her earlier when I knew we had to move again."

Tori nodded.

Katelyn's long brown hair pulled back in a flattering ponytail, she flashed a brilliant smile, letting them know she was teasing. "Hey, Tori. It's good to see you, though I'd prefer it were under much different circumstances."

Tori looked from Ryan to Katelyn. So he'd brought in a chaperone? He didn't trust himself to be alone with Tori? Oh, she wished that thought hadn't even occurred to her.

"It's nice to see you, too. So why exactly are you here, if I may ask?" The question sounded kind of rude, but she wanted to know what was going on.

"I can see those wheels spinning in your head." Ryan's wink brought on a blush.

That he could read her mind made her cheeks all the warmer.

Ryan cleared his throat. "Katelyn can take you where you need to go, if you actually *need* to get out. Let's hope we get this guy, and soon. Things seem to be ramping up."

"You mean whoever killed Sarah is becoming desperate to find and kill me for whatever they think I know. Their actions seem counterintuitive to me. Escalating the murder attempts only increases the heat on them."

Arms crossed, he nodded. "Agreed. But it doesn't seem likely the guy is going to back down now, even if he could better protect himself by hiding rather than attacking. In the meantime, we're on the lookout for the two vehicles that approached the original safe house, so I hope we get a hit there. Jasper has security cameras so we can use those to see if we can get more details. But if solving this case takes much longer, then we'll have to make different arrangements for you—that is, unless you're willing to go back to your job on the other side of the country."

Katelyn appeared thoughtful, her blue-green gaze startlingly similar to Ryan's.

"I'm here to help you, Tori," Katelyn said. "As a friend, of course, but also to help out my twin brother. But I should mention he's paying me, too." She offered a silly grin. "I'm freelancing right now."

"Freelancing?" Katelyn worked in law enforcement in the town of Shasta, Tori had thought. What happened to that?

"Let's just say I'm in between law enforcement jobs." Katelyn lifted her jacket to reveal she was armed, then unpacked the groceries. Looked like they were eating Italian tonight. "And I can also cook a mean pot of pasta."

Tori chuckled. "Well, this should be interesting."

Ryan opened the fridge. "Three heads are better than two."

"Three heads?" Tori asked. "What about your entire sheriff's department? What about the FBI?"

"When it comes to you, Tori," he said, "I'm holding your safety close."

Meaning this time, no one besides Ryan and his twin sister knew where Tori was staying. That is, unless someone had followed them here. Maybe someone had followed them to the last house, despite their best efforts to conceal their travel destination.

"Fair enough."

Ryan had grabbed three sodas and set them on the counter. "You thirsty?"

"Sure, but…" She shifted the purse on her shoulder and eyed her duffel and laptop case. "Can I put my things somewhere?"

He studied Tori for a moment, the hint of his grin barely revealing his dimples. "Pardon my manners. You'll find the guest bedroom down the hallway. Second door to the right."

Tori found the room decorated in shades of sage and brown. Comforting and practical. Had Katelyn been the decorator? When Tori and Ryan had dated years ago, he hadn't owned a house. He'd lived in an apartment.

An image flashed through her thoughts of her and Ryan together. Married. Living in a home of their own, busy and active with their law enforcement careers. A small framed picture sat on the side table. She lifted it to get a closer look. The picture was older and portrayed his parents and siblings—they were all much younger. Ryan was probably only ten.

Kids.

Sarah had wanted that life. She'd wanted to get married and have a family.

Tori had kept pushing that part of her dream further out each year. She might have even put it off until it was too late. She chewed on her lip. Focusing on her career first had made sense at the time...but Sarah's death had changed her perspective and, in fact, was still changing the way Tori viewed life. The way she viewed everything.

Ryan.

She set the picture down. What about Ryan's brothers? What were they doing now? Oh, why was she feeling so nostalgic when there was work to be done? Tori shoved the mushy feelings over to the far side of her heart so she could concentrate on helping Ryan get to the bottom of this.

Plus, Tori had a decision to make. Should she ask for a longer leave and stay or go all the way and give up her job? Or when her bereavement leave was up, should she go back to her job and leave Ryan to find Sarah's killer and Tori's attacker without her help? Thoughts of stepping away from the investigation left her unsettled. Not that she didn't trust him, but she was worried about him, too. The killer had already murdered five people. If Tori got far enough away, she should be safe, but Ryan would still be here in the midst of it. Touching the image of a young Ryan in the photograph, she pursed her lips.

Uncertainty weighed on her, though she needed to make a decision. She would need to know the answer to her own questions soon.

She left her duffel and purse on the queen bed and snatched her laptop from the case. She brought it with her back into the kitchen and set it on the table. Katelyn had already filled the room with the delicious smells of Italian food. Tori's stomach rumbled in response.

"Where's Ryan?" she asked.

"He's on a call. Something about the FBI and ecoterrorists." Katelyn gestured toward the front part of the house.

"Good." That meant they wouldn't lose more time than they'd already lost today. She crept forward, not to eavesdrop, but to let him know she was available to participate if needed.

She saw him standing there, cell to his ear as he peeked through the mini blinds, out the front window. For a few seconds she studied his profile. A strong jaw and well-defined masculine features. A few whiskers had erupted on his cheek where he shaved to form the Vandyke beard. Finally he turned his head to look at her, as though he'd been aware of her presence all along. He didn't appear disturbed with her for intruding on his call.

"I understand," he spoke into the cell. "Yep. We'll be there."

He ended the call.

"We'll be there?" she asked. "What's going on?"

"I just spoke with an FBI agent. He sounded perturbed with us. We're meeting with him in twenty."

"What?" Hands fisted on her hips, Katelyn stared at them as she strolled into the room. "And miss my pasta? I was cooking it up special, just for you."

Ryan chuckled and glanced at his smartphone. "If it's ready we can eat fast and make it."

"No way," she said. "You do your meeting and then we'll have a nice relaxed meal when you get back. No rushing through a meal I'm taking my time to make." Katelyn leaned close to Tori and squeezed her arm. "Besides, I want to catch up with Tori."

Tori and Katelyn had been friendly, but not all that close. Still, Katelyn's friendliness warmed her. With Sarah gone, Tori's heart ached with loneliness, and even the smallest of gestures meant so much.

"I'd like that, too," Tori said.

"That'll work, then," Ryan said. "I don't think we'll be that long." Ryan glanced at Tori.

"The plan for coming and going will always be the same. You have to duck down in the vehicle before I exit the garage. Wear the cap and the wig, just in case."

Tori stared at the ceiling and shook her head. "Like that worked so well the last time. Whoever is looking for me is not going to be fooled."

"We do all we know to do, Tori. Just work with me on this, okay?"

"Okay, fine. Let's do this."

Ryan sat in the passenger seat of the special agent's big black SUV parked under the overpass of a bridge in an abandoned industrial area. The agent remained in the driver's seat. Tori sat in the back seat. This clandestine meeting was like something from a movie. Ryan didn't like it.

Why couldn't they be up front and out in the open?

His cell had buzzed a few times. His captain was calling him.

Special Agent Sanchez remained stoic, but Ryan suspected that beneath the surface he was fuming. "Sarah Peterson's murder had nothing to do with her involvement in the ecoterrorist group."

"You can't know that. I think you're trying to

deflect your responsibility in this." Tori wasn't hiding her own frustration.

"Ecoterrorists aren't profiled as murderers. The extent of their activism typically involves property damage. Sarah's murder was part of a multiple homicide. Your investigation has taken a wrong turn, Detective."

"How do you explain Dee James's murder?" Tori asked. "He was murdered because he knew something about Sarah."

"I'm sorry, are you investigating, Special Agent Peterson? Because it was my understanding you're on bereavement leave." Sanchez's unemotional features suddenly shifted. He was losing his patience. "What's going on, Detective Bradley?"

"I'm in charge of this investigation," Ryan said. "Since Tori has insight into her sister that we wouldn't otherwise have, I've asked her to offer her expertise. Her knowledge of her sister's life led us to Sarah's involvement with Dee James, which led us to her email alias, and then finally to you."

"You were not led to me. I contacted you because you could have cost us months of work. Do you know that?" Now was the moment when the agent would come unhinged.

Instead, he blew out a breath. "We took down the ecoterrorist activists within A Better World at four this morning. We raided the homes of eight people and brought charges against them for planning to bomb a factory."

"But not murder?"

"No. But if we learn more about Sarah's death from our perpetrators, you can learn about that on the news. Now if you'll excuse me, I have someplace to be."

"Wait, Special Agent Sanchez," Tori said. "Please tell me that Sarah wasn't involved in violence. That she wasn't an ecoterrorist who got caught and had to make a deal."

He pursed his lips for a couple of breaths, then said, "She was working with us the whole time, Peterson, if that eases your mind. As for her murder, I suggest you get back on track with your investigation, Detective, and focus on a different target and motive. You've missed the boat on this one."

The agent was dismissing them.

Ryan suspected that Tori wanted to argue more. How could the arrogant Agent Sanchez know that someone within A Better World hadn't found out that Sarah was an informant and decided to take revenge? Did Dee James know what Sarah was up to? Tori made it sound as if the guy liked Sarah and wanted to help. But Sarah had taken his idea of an alias email and used it against him.

He stood with Tori under the bridge and watched Sanchez drive away in his slick black Suburban. Again, just like in the movies.

"Well, that was weird," Tori said.

Ryan would keep his thoughts to himself for the moment.

Back in his county vehicle, Ryan started the ignition, and let Tori process the meeting, as well. Ryan said nothing as he absorbed the news shared by the agent.

Tori pressed her head against the seat back and released a soft sigh. "It could be over, then. They've arrested the main threats in the group and will obviously find out more by questioning them. The FBI will know if there was some reason they could have had to kill Sarah, her friends, and then also Dee. I just know that Dee was scared. If only he had shared everything he knew with me. But maybe someone in this group they've arrested will share more—like who found me at the safe house today."

"I hope you're right." For Tori's safety's sake. "Let's hope they discover the true reasons for Sarah's murder now that they have made some arrests, but it doesn't sound like they're connecting those dots the same way we are. I'll do what I can to find out more, even though this guy made it clear he wasn't going to share the information with us. Maybe when your leave is over, you can somehow use your connections within the FBI to find out more."

"You're assuming that I'm going back to work for them. I told you that I was considering staying even if only by extending my leave. You didn't believe me?"

"No, actually. I believed you would come to your senses."

"Can we just get out of here?" Irritation edged her tone.

"Yes." He glanced at her. "But first, pull your cap on."

She flicked her green eyes his way, and though she tried to send him a severe look, dimples broke out on her cheeks. And at the sight of them, his heart was in his throat. He reined in his emotions before he spoke.

"Tori, please. You agreed to work with me."

"Fine, but I'm not ducking." She tucked the hat over the wig of long black hair. "Even if Sanchez believes the killer is still out there, since he doesn't believe the activists murdered her."

"We can't know for sure, and I, for one, don't want to take any chances. There are too many unanswered questions." He steered from the parking lot. "So let's do this. Let's relax and eat with Katelyn when we get back to my house. She's going to be upset if we don't, I know that much. So please just try to enjoy the dinner that she cooked. Sometimes we have to get away from the investigation long enough to clear our heads."

"Agreed. And I assure you I won't have to work hard to enjoy her dinner. It smelled amazing. Besides, I need a break. I've been overthinking. Whatever Agent Sanchez says, I still believe Sarah's murder has something to do with that group—or at least her environmental activities, which just leads back to them. Maybe there's another group she was involved with. Something we missed. At least the ecoterrorist faction has been effectively shut down for the time being. But after I eat Katelyn's pasta, who knows what I will think."

God, please let this be over.

And if it truly was over—if Tori was right and Agent Sanchez was wrong—then she would probably go back to her job in South Carolina. Maybe she wouldn't go back now, or even next week, but eventually. His throat threatened to close up on him at the thought.

"Look out!"

Tori screamed.

The vehicle filled his vision. He accelerated and swerved in hopes of a near miss. But he had no time to escape the vehicle as it slammed into them.

THIRTEEN

A loud blast filled her ears as a force propelled her forward. The next thing Tori knew, she sat in the vehicle, stunned, a deflated airbag in her lap and a weird smell filling the air. Seconds ticked by before she shook off the daze and gathered her wits. The airbag had exploded and the impact happened much too fast for her to comprehend.

And screams.

She'd heard screams.

Tori realized the screams had come from her. But she wasn't screaming now. She was absorbing the fact they'd been in a car crash and she was still alive. She gasped for much-needed oxygen as her heart pounded. Dizziness tried to swallow her but she fought it. She remembered a vehicle had headed straight for them.

A hand gripped her. "Tori. Are you hurt?"

Ryan. Ryan had been driving.

"No, I'm not hurt. I'm… I'm okay." She

looked at him, a deflated airbag in his lap as well, but he had a cut across his forehead, and the sunglasses propped on his head were broken. "But *you're* hurt."

She touched his head and then looked at the blood on her fingertips. Ryan checked the rearview mirror that barely remained intact on the cracked windshield. "I'll live. We have to get out of here."

Tori reached up to touch her own head to see if she, too, was bleeding. Then she realized she was no longer wearing the wig. The impact had dislodged the disguise she'd donned moments before. She disentangled herself from the airbag and unbuckled the seat belt to search for the wig. The move ignited a throb across her chest. She'd have a bruise from the seat belt, if not the airbag.

"Get ready to run." Ryan's tone was urgent. "Tori, are you listening?"

"Sure." She tried to shake off the daze.

"I need you to stay down until I can get you out." Ryan grabbed her chin and forced her to look at him. "The wreck was deliberate. Your life is in jeopardy." Ryan had his weapon out. "Get down, please."

He urged her downward in the seat, which was hard because the front end was crunched inward, giving her less room. Again her chest throbbed. Tori did her best to remain down and out of view.

"Wait here," he said. "I'll be back."

Ryan tried to open his door, but it wouldn't budge. He shoved against it repeatedly. Then he shifted his body around, putting himself practically over her, and kicked the door open. He slipped out of the vehicle.

"We should stay together, Ryan."

But he was gone. What was he doing? Panic spiked through her. Tori tried the passenger door. It wouldn't budge. She reached for her own gun.

She could possibly crawl over the console and out of Ryan's opened side, but then that would expose her if someone was aiming to shoot her. Tori remained crunched down in the seat.

Gunshots exploded around her in an exchange. Between Ryan and who else? Was he up against one person or many?

Her breathing accelerated. She needed to help him.

I have to get out of here. I'm a sitting duck.

"Where are you, Ryan?"

With all the gunfire, he could be shot and injured or worse… Dead.

He'd told her to wait, but she couldn't.

Then she heard him.

"Tori, get out of the vehicle! I can't make it to you!" he called, his voice sounding distant. "I'll hold him off!"

More gunshots resounded.

Time to move.

She kicked against her door again but it still wouldn't budge. Tori crawled across the console to the driver's side. Keeping low, she slid out, her weapon ready to fire. She needed somewhere to go, but she was stuck hiding behind the door of the vehicle as she tried to figure out where to go. She wanted to call out to Ryan but didn't want to give herself away. He had to know she had climbed out, because he'd been shooting at someone to keep them from shooting at her.

If someone wanted her dead, wasn't there any easier way to go about it? What a ridiculous thought to have at this moment.

Footfalls pounded the ground.

Two sets now.

Her heart hammered. Someone was running, but in which direction? Away from her, or toward her? She risked a peek down the alley and spotted Ryan giving chase.

That was it. She was going, too. Tori shoved from the vehicle, propelling herself forward and running after the two of them. The man he was chasing turned a corner.

"Ryan, wait up!" she called.

Ryan hesitated at the corner and then turned to wait for her. She caught up with him and didn't miss a step as together they bounded around the corner and into the service vehicle access behind the buildings.

But the guy had disappeared. They continued forward until they made the end of the access behind the buildings that opened up to another alley.

She gasped for breath. "Déjà vu. This happened before. We can't lose him this time. I'm going right, and you go left."

"No." Ryan held his weapon ready to aim and fire at the first sign of trouble. "We'll go together."

Tori didn't argue and crept down the alley, Ryan at her side. She held her weapon ready to lift and fire at a moment's notice. As she moved, she looked in every direction, waiting for the perp to jump out of the shadows or a corner. Ryan did the same but she had the uncanny sense that he was guarding her, as well. What a strange situation to be thrust into. At least Tori trusted Ryan to have her back, though she wasn't giving him much choice at the moment.

A door slammed in a vacant building up ahead. She gestured toward the building. "In there."

"I don't like this, Tori," Ryan said.

"I don't like it, either, but we have to catch

this guy. I'm not going to be safe until this is over." Clearly she'd been completely wrong to believe she was safe with the ecoterrorist group in custody. Sanchez had been right on that point. That chafed. Unless Sanchez had been wrong and they had missed someone. But she couldn't think about that right now.

Ryan grabbed her before she entered. "I'm lead on this. I'll give chase."

"And I'll watch your back."

He opened the door and stepped inside. "Police. Give it up."

Slowly and methodically they cleared rooms on the lower level of a forsaken, multi-floor commercial building, then moved to the next floor. Neither of them spoke as they worked together. Very well together, she noted.

When they approached the last door in the building, Ryan hesitated and they shared a knowing look. The guy had to be in this room. And the perp had to know this was the end of the line for him.

Ryan positioned himself to safely enter the room, then called out in his official law enforcement tone, "It's all over. I'm going to open the door. If you're holding a weapon—"

The man fired off three shots. Bullets passed through the door. Tori's pulse roared in her ears.

"I think he's out," Ryan said.

"He could have another clip," she said.

Ryan nodded. "Give it up," he called through to the shooter. "I'm with the Maynor County Sheriff's Office, and I'm going to open this door. I'm going to shoot you if you are still holding a weapon. Understand?"

"Understood." The response from behind the door surprised her.

Except, what did that really mean?

"Be careful, Ryan," she said. "This could be a trap."

Ryan kicked the door open and pointed his weapon. "Police!"

Tori came in low behind him.

A man stood at the far side of the room with his hands in his air. A gun lay on the floor in front of him. "I'm out, man. Don't shoot me. I'm out." Oddly, tears leaked from his eyes.

He was scared? That didn't fit with the cold-blooded killer she'd been imagining. There was more going on here than she'd realized.

Finally a break in this case. The break they needed. Finally she could learn what happened to Sarah.

The window shattered. The perp's face scrunched and then he crumpled as gunfire rang out.

* * *

Lights flashed from the emergency vehicles parked near the car accident that had taken out Ryan's unmarked car. The wrecked vehicles had been moved to the side of the road to allow for traffic to flow.

The county coroner had already examined the perp's body, and the building across the street from where the kill shot had been fired had been swept for evidence. Ryan hadn't been informed on what had been discovered yet.

Medics had checked both Ryan and Tori out because neither of them wanted to sit in the hospital again. Not with a killer out there. With the attacks ramping up, they had to be getting close to the truth about who was behind this. And that meant Tori was in even more danger.

Ryan and Tori had already given their statements. It was getting late and Ryan was exhausted, but he'd grown somewhat accustomed to the long and odd hours as a detective. What was unfamiliar—and uncomfortable—was the hands-on scrutiny he was facing. Ryan shifted back and forth on his aching feet as he filled in his boss, Captain Moran, as well as his boss's superiors, Chief Deputy Carmichael and Sheriff Rollins. It was a rough day when the heads of the sheriff's department came to the scene of the crime to question Ryan on the events of the evening, including the clandestine meeting with the FBI agent. Sheriff Rollins was none too happy about the turn in Ryan's investigation, the threats on Tori's life or the FBI agent's attitude.

Ryan's investigative tactics were being scrutinized, as well, for everyone to hear. Couldn't they take this back to the office to discuss?

"I get the feeling from you that Special Agent Peterson has been working this investigation, perhaps even leading you, the lead detective on the case," Captain Moran said.

The chief deputy watched and listened.

Ryan knew when to speak, and when to keep quiet. Now wasn't the time to reply. His boss hadn't finished with him.

"Maybe I need to have a few words with Agent Peterson's boss," Sheriff Rollins said. "It's time for her to leave. She's a distraction to you, Ryan, and her life's in danger, and almost cost you yours."

"Where is she now?" Captain Moran asked.

Ryan was more than relieved Katelyn had picked Tori up and carted her away from the scene so she wouldn't have to endure more questions. "Safe."

The captain eyed him. "I asked you a question, Detective."

"In light of the fact that someone knew where

to look for her at my original safe house," Ryan said, "I prefer not sharing her location information here." He gestured to the law enforcement presence and the public gathered at the scene. "Add to that, the Jeep that slammed into us was seen at the original safe house."

Captain Moran lost his tough stance, his features softening a bit. Ryan hadn't known him to be harsh, but maybe the captain was under pressure with his two superiors here, as well. He had to perform his duties or be scrutinized himself.

"That was the correct response," he said. "Lets me know that you've got your head on straight."

Tension eased from Ryan's shoulders.

"Yes, sir," Ryan said. "We have the name of the man who was driving and who was subsequently shot and killed. Eddie Slattery. We've run a background. I'm still looking for his connection to the other murders—of Sarah Peterson and her friends, and Dee James. Or a connection to anyone who would want to harm Tori."

The sheriff nodded, only half listening as he answered his cell.

Ryan released a slow sigh of relief. He fisted his hands by his sides, impatient to finish the inquisition and answer their questions—all of which would be written up in his reports for them to read later. He understood the investigation of four murders, now six, had taken several turns and the public also wanted the killer caught. The entire sheriff's office was being scrutinized, not just Ryan as the lead investigator.

But all he wanted, all he could think about was to get out of here and check on Tori. They needed to talk through the implications of what happened tonight. This could mean they had been following the wrong leads. Did Sarah's murder have something to do with her social justice activities or not?

Captain Moran squeezed Ryan's shoulder. "All right. I think we're done here. Carry on, Detective Bradley. You're doing a good job staying on top of things, considering all that's happened so far. But I do agree with the sheriff that Sarah's sister needs to be out of the investigation."

"She has insight into her sister's goings-on and has provided me with important information."

"I understand. She's offering assistance, but she's also interfering with your investigation,

I hope you realize that. When is she heading home to her real job again?"

"I'm not sure. I've tried to persuade her to leave."

"Well, try harder." With those words Captain Moran left him, to join the sheriff and chief deputy.

Captain Moran had effectively dismissed him. That was fine, because he wanted to leave and find Tori.

Except, to get out of here, he was going to need a new vehicle.

His cell buzzed. He looked at the text.

To your right.

Ryan turned and spotted Katelyn's car parked a distance away from the wreck. He jogged over and climbed in on the passenger side, painfully aware that Tori was not in the vehicle with his sister.

He stiffened. "What's going on? Why aren't you guarding Tori like I'm paying you to?"

She steered the vehicle around the corner. "I can't protect someone who doesn't want to be protected. When we got back to your house, Tori called a cab and left."

FOURTEEN

Tori dropped her briefcase, duffel and purse on one of two queen beds in the airport motel. She still couldn't comprehend the chain of events that had propelled her here.

Maybe she had this all wrong.

Maybe she shouldn't have walked away from Ryan's attempt at protection. But someone had seemed to know their every move, no matter what they did. And this evening, Ryan had almost been killed along with Tori. Sure, he was accustomed to dangerous situations, but like he told her—it was harder to stay safe when someone was targeting you, even if you were trained law enforcement.

Tori might not have listened to his words before, but they hit harder when it concerned Ryan. After the deliberate car crash, she made the decision she wouldn't put him or his sister in the line of fire. She'd already lost her own sister. The Bradley family didn't need to lose anyone because of Tori.

Besides, she was due back in the office the day after tomorrow. If she returned to her job, it would take her a day of travel and recovery at her apartment as it was. Uncertainty about her plans had plagued her for the last few days, but now she knew exactly what she would do.

She would go back to South Carolina and hope she could find out more about Sarah's murder when she was back at work. Right now, it was time to get her things ready for flying. Tori dumped her purse to clear it of anything that wouldn't clear security, and she spotted a small round device. She lifted it to examine it.

A GPS tracker.

Tori groaned.

"Idiot! I'm such a stupid idiot."

A knock came at the door. Panic swelled in her chest and she gripped her weapon. Tori didn't ask who it was, she simply waited quietly in case it was the man who had shot Eddie Slattery—the perp who'd drive his Jeep into them and shot at them. She'd just found a GPS—was that his? Had he somehow gotten access to her things to plant the tracker and then followed her here where she was all alone?

Sweat beaded on her temple.

"It's me."

Ryan.

Tori released a slow breath.

Ryan's tone wasn't gruff like she would expect, but instead he sounded...desperate? Whatever. She was both relieved and perturbed. Him finding Tori here meant one thing. She marched to the door and opened it, leaving it wide for Ryan to enter. He shut it behind him.

She held the GPS tracker up for him to see. "Really?"

He shrugged. "That wasn't me."

"Katelyn." Tori squeezed her temples. "How could I have been so stupid?"

Ryan's sister had advised Tori against leaving, at least until she could talk it out with Ryan. Katelyn had known that Ryan would be furious with the both of them—Tori for leaving and Katelyn for allowing it. Tori had known that, too, but at the time she hadn't cared. She was thinking about their safety. Tori had gotten into the back seat of the cab with her laptop and Katelyn had handed off her duffel and purse. She would have had the opportunity to place the tracker then. Katelyn had been thinking ahead. She was a smart cookie.

"She wanted to make sure you were okay," he said. "That you got to the airport safely."

"And that you could find me."

Leaning against the wall, Ryan crossed his

arms. "Right. She meant to help, that's all. What if something happened to you, Tori? You're in danger. Running off like this wasn't a smart move."

"And you think the tracker would help you to find me if I were abducted or left for dead? If the bad guys nabbed me, I don't think they would let me bring my purse." She sent him a wry grin.

"You might have found a way to convince the nabber you needed to keep it. That said, he might still look inside, so you'd need a backup tracker." Ryan responded with his own grin.

"No…" Katelyn hadn't! Tori shrugged out of her jacket and searched. She removed her shoes and looked inside and out.

"Relax. I don't know if that's the only tracker Katelyn planted, but we do know that someone has known where you've been. Like the bedroom in Sarah's house."

"And the first safe house—the dream house."

"And like tonight. Eddie drove that Jeep right for you. He aimed at your side of the vehicle. I couldn't stop the collision but I tried to swerve so he wouldn't crush the passenger side." He scraped a hand down his face as it paled.

The implication got to him as it did her. A chill crawled over her.

She palmed her weapon. "And you think they could have followed me here."

"I think if you're heading back home then you shouldn't stay here tonight. You should get an earlier flight and wait in the airport beyond the security checkpoints. Take the red-eye, even. I'm happy to take you to the airport. But if you're not going to stay with me, then go there and be safe. You know you're not safe until whoever is behind this is caught."

"Unfortunately, I do know that." Tori sat on the edge of the bed. "Listen, I'm sorry I left without at least saying goodbye. I just didn't want to endanger you or your sister, or anyone who is near me."

He gave her a look, and then she suddenly remembered his words to her—he'd told her that she would go back. She was glad he didn't say, "I told you so."

"So yes, you were right about me, after all. I'm not staying here like I had been considering. I think I can do a better job finding answers for us if I'm back at work and can gain access to information we need. Special Agent Sanchez isn't going to share with you, that much is clear. I don't even know if I can get anyone to share with *me* even if I put pressure on them from within, but I'm going to work that angle. Katelyn will be safe because she won't have to protect me. I don't want you to be in danger, either." Tori didn't want to keep having to dodge bombs and bullets until this was over.

"She's pretty miffed at you, you know. She would have helped me protect you for nothing, but she needed the work." He frowned.

"You don't need to lose your sister, too, especially because of me. Besides, it's not just her I'm worried about. You could have died tonight, too. This way, you won't be in danger, either—at least, not because of me."

Her words surprised herself. She hadn't realized how deeply she cared for Ryan's safety. But her worry for him hadn't only been about his safety. Her concern took her through forbidden territory. She and Ryan already had their chance at something special once before.

"You know that comes with the job, right? And if you're worried about Katelyn, if that's why you're leaving, then we can do something about that. Because... I'm the one who's supposed to protect you." Now his tone had turned gruff.

Maybe he'd been right in the first place—about leaving. She'd go to the airport and hang out there. See about getting an earlier flight. She began stuffing everything back into her bag.

"You're confusing me, Ryan. You've continued to insist that I leave. Insist that I go home where I'll be safer. Now you sound like you want me to stay. The truth is, I'm only a distraction to your investigation. That's all I've ever been. You need to focus. I'm sorry, I thought I could help."

He stepped closer.

That made her heart beat all the harder.

"You *have* helped." Deep need resonated through his tone.

Tori fought her trembling hands. "No. I sent us both in the wrong direction."

"But Dee James knew something," he said. "That was not the wrong direction."

"I think… I think he was truly concerned for Sarah's safety and Dee was killed for the same reason someone is trying to kill me. For something they thought he knew. Something they think *I* know. And now tonight the guy who followed me to the safe house and who rammed us, another of our leads in addition to Dee James, is dead."

Ryan took a step toward her, as if he wasn't already much too close. "Tori…"

Her heart skipped around inside at the way he said her name. She pressed her fingers over her eyes. "I can't think clearly with you standing so close."

In the room.

In the house.

In her life.

She huffed out a breath. "Just… I need to go. You were right all along. I shouldn't have stayed. I've only messed everything up."

"Tori, I—"

She avoided looking at his face or into his eyes. That was the only way she could keep from melting right into his arms. "Go, Ryan. I'll call a cab. I can take care of myself."

Her words had the wanted effect. He took a step back. "I'll wait until I see the cab pick you up."

"Fine. Do what you need to do."

Still, she didn't look at him as she moved to peek through the door and window to make sure it was safe to exit. Then she held the door open for him, hating this whole scene—but she had to be cold and calculated to let him go.

For herself and for him.

Finally she lifted her gaze to meet his. Ryan studied her, then his striking features turned severe. "Safe travels, Tori. I hope you'll share with me anything you learn."

He turned his back on her and exited the room.

Tori shut the door and leaned against it. She calmed her breathing. The room seemed to spin a little and felt lonely and empty with him gone. She'd been fine before he'd shown up. Hadn't she?

She concentrated on getting her act together and getting herself to the airport. Once she was back on the job, she would be safer.

At least, Ryan had kept telling her that, and now she believed it, too.

She needed distance between herself and her attacker—and access to the FBI's resources. That was the best way to catch this guy. She wouldn't truly be safe until she'd discovered whatever this person thought she knew, and then she would take him down.

I'm coming for you!

Tori dug through all her belongings in search of another possible tracking device—Katelyn's or someone else's. Her belongings seemed clean. Not that it mattered, since Ryan knew exactly where she was at the moment. She had no doubt that he would follow the cab to the airport, and that was his choice, but she wouldn't ride in a vehicle with him again and put him in danger.

She wouldn't stay here any longer and put her heart in danger, either.

Ryan had borrowed Katelyn's vehicle and waited inside. He'd have to pick up a new one tomorrow at the office when he went in to file reports. He really didn't have time for all the paperwork, with everything going on.

Like now. He should be back at the station, writing up his reports, but instead, he watched the motel near the airport for signs of suspicious activity. Anyone who might be sitting and waiting on Tori, like he was.

Waiting on Tori.

Had that been what he'd been doing for the last several years? Had he been keeping busy with his job and pretending to find satisfaction in that while deep inside, he secretly hoped and waited for the day when Tori would come back to him? Pathetic. He'd let her go, and like the adage claimed, if she came back to him then she was his. And now that she was, in fact, back, had Ryan been harboring a hope that Tori would stay because of him? That she wanted to be with him?

He rubbed his eyes to push back the ridiculous thoughts. His reaction to her cutting out on him blindsided him. He should have been encouraging her to leave instead of desperately trying to keep her here. His motivations were purely selfish. He'd own that, sure. But they'd worked together well, he thought, and they could *still* work together well once on the other side of this investigation. When Sarah's killer was caught and Tori was safe and sound.

That had been a secret dream of his long ago—the two of them solving crimes together, and going home together. But she'd taken a different path.

Together until death do us part.

He coughed up a chuckle. Ryan truly loathed himself at this moment. A few more seconds and he might have found himself begging her to stay. It all proved to be a real eye-opener regarding his own character.

He could berate himself in the weeks and months to come, but right now he focused back on the situation. He had to keep Tori safe while she headed to the airport. He didn't blame her for not wanting to ride with him.

Twenty minutes later a cab pulled into the parking lot.

Ryan stiffened. If someone had followed her here, this could be the moment they took action.

He started his vehicle and watched her get into the cab. The white minivan then steered slowly through the parking lot, which seemed to take an eternity. Ryan just wanted her at the airport—checked in and through security, where she would be safest.

Finally the cab turned onto the street and Ryan followed closely behind, hoping to provide a deterrence to anyone who thought about attacking her again.

The cab's driver seemed to inch along the freeway and Ryan thought about calling Tori to have her ask the man to speed things up. But she'd made it clear she could and would take care of herself. Ryan followed the cab around the airport drive. Then he pulled up behind it when the cab stopped in front of the drop-off. Ryan didn't get out but simply watched from the inside of Katelyn's vehicle.

He watched Tori, waiting for the moment when she would glance back at him. He planned to give her a little wave. He also planned to follow her inside—from a distance. But she didn't look back as she carried her duffel and laptop case into the terminal. Ryan left Katelyn's vehicle at the drop-off zone and followed Tori inside. Until she was through the security gate, someone could still cause her problems. Even after she was through, they could try to harm her, but the chances were much lower considering no unauthorized personnel could carry a weapon through the security screening.

Inside the terminal, he stood back and watched and waited. If Tori knew he'd followed her inside, she didn't let on. That she didn't acknowledge him squeezed his heart, leaving him sick to his stomach.

Get a grip, man. Why had he let her get so deeply under his skin again?

Finally she moved through the security gate. He would have expected to breathe a sigh of relief, except he'd just let the love of his life get away from him again.

He made his way back to Katelyn's vehicle, which he'd left illegally parked. Captain Moran called and Ryan gave him an update, relieved he could actually tell his captain that Tori was at the airport, waiting to board a plane. When he approached his vehicle, an airport cop was writing him a ticket. Ryan flashed his Maynor County Sheriff's detective badge and explained his business and then got in.

Katelyn called as he pulled away.

He answered with "No, your vehicle isn't wrecked. And yes, Tori is at the airport, checked through security. I'm heading home now."

"I wasn't calling to check up on you. Not really. You can take care of yourself, little brother."

"Hey, I'm not your little brother just because I was born two minutes after you."

"Uh-huh." Katelyn chuckled. "I was calling because I've found an interesting connection that you're going to want to look into."

FIFTEEN

Tori found a seat at the gate. She would go standby on the next flight back to South Carolina, which included a lot of connections. Still, that didn't take off for another three hours, so this could very well turn into a long night. She decided she would put that time to good use, doing the same thing she would do in the motel room, only here she wouldn't be constantly listening for someone approaching the door.

She could easily spot an approaching threat from where she sat at the gate, her back to the window and facing the inside of the terminal.

Ryan had been right to suggest she hang out at the airport, though part of her felt like a coward. But she didn't want to die before she could solve the mystery of who killed Sarah. That person needed to pay for what he'd done to six people now, adding Dee James and Eddie Slattery to the group.

Sorrow for their loss left her hollowed out.

If she and Ryan had solved the first murders sooner, then the others might still be alive.

Or…if Sarah hadn't gotten involved in something that turned her into a target, all six people might still be alive. But it did no good to take that perspective.

While she waited to gain access to the flight home, she could work on her laptop. She sent her supervisor an email, notifying him that she was returning and would be back in the office tomorrow. She also thanked him for the flowers the department had sent for Sarah's funeral, though she planned to send a handwritten note, as well. She had to tread carefully in how she explained the FBI's possible connection to her sister's death. She tried to focus on how best to word her email, but her thoughts kept going back to Ryan.

She'd been painfully aware of his vehicle following the cab, and that he'd gotten out and followed her inside, watching until she made it through security. A thousand times she'd considered approaching him or at least acknowledging his presence, but what would that solve? Nothing. It would only stir up the same old argument of whether she should stay or whether she should go, and those same unwanted emotions would erupt.

She had to put what being with Ryan for the

last few days had stirred inside her back into a locked box. She sent an email to Dad, letting him know of her departure and why she'd had to leave. Tori explained that she would be back for a short visit or they could come out to see her, once the person responsible for Sarah's death and Tori's attacks was incarcerated. He would be hurt that he didn't at least get to say goodbye in person—which was the reason she chose to email rather than get into the emotional drama over the phone—but he would have to understand. He would then break the news to Mom. Together, they would console themselves with the fact that Tori was doing what they had wanted her to do, and that she would be safer. They wouldn't lose another daughter.

Tori sat taller and shoved the sudden tears away.

She let the fury at this killer wash through her and leave her as a force to be reckoned with.

Dad replied to her email sooner than she would have thought, stating that he was glad she would be safe and he looked forward to hearing from her when she arrived. Phew. Relieved at his response, she read more. He said they would discuss coming out for a visit when she had time.

And that was another issue, wasn't it? In her

job she hardly had time for family, especially when she lived halfway across the country.

Her cell rang.

Mom.

Tori flinched. Mom would stir up her emotions, and she needed to stay levelheaded as she remained on guard.

Groaning inside, she answered the call. "Mom, hi."

"Hey, honey. I know you can't tell me where you are, where the safe house is. I understand all that, but I wanted to hear your voice. I miss you."

Disappointment sank in Tori's gut—Dad hadn't told Mom the news yet. Her mother could very well figure her location out when she heard the background noise. Tori pinched the bridge of her nose, wishing now that she hadn't answered. Why hadn't she simply let it go to voice mail?

"I miss you, too, Mom. Let's pray this is over soon and we can spend time together without having to worry."

"I can't lose you, too, Tori." Mom's words sounded warbled, but Tori suspected she was doing her best to control her emotions.

"You won't, Mom. I promise." She might as well go ahead and tell her she was leaving.

"I meant to ask, what was in that package Sarah sent you?"

Package?

"What package?"

"You didn't find it? It came to our house a few days ago—they forwarded it from your apartment. I stuck it in your briefcase when they gathered your things from Sarah's house. That was after the explosion. You were in the hospital."

"Right. They took me to the safe house from there. I didn't see a package, but I haven't rifled through my briefcase—" though she had pulled her laptop out of its pocket several times "—Listen, Mom, I have—"

An announcement for an incoming flight came over the intercom.

"Where are you, Tori? It sounds like you're at the airport. What's going on?"

Air whooshed from Tori's lungs. "I'm heading home, Mom. I emailed Dad to explain that in order to be safe, I need to leave."

"But—"

Mom would have at least wanted to see her off. To say goodbye. Give her a hug. Tori got it. This wasn't how Mom had imagined Tori going somewhere safe.

Dad's voice sounded in the background as

he explained to Mom what was going on. *A little late, Dad.*

She'd wanted to avoid the drama. While she listened to the secondhand conversation, she dug through her briefcase and spotted a small package—the one from Sarah?

"Mom, I think I found the package. I have to go." Tori ended the call abruptly. Mom would have to understand, and Tori would make up for it later.

Gripping the orange-colored mailer, she stared at the handwriting—Sarah's writing—and the date it had been sent. The day before Sarah's murder. Tori had made sure to forward her mail to Mom and Dad's, and it had taken time to find her here.

Without a doubt she knew what she held in her hands was the information that had put a target on her head. They thought that she already knew. That she had already received the package.

She slid it over her keyboard to hide it behind her laptop and looked around the terminal. The rush and madness to make the next flight had died down and only one person sat in the waiting area with her. Few people walked the halls.

Tori ripped the package and a USB drive fell out. She peeked inside the package and found a sealed envelope, too. She opened it to find a handwritten note from Sarah.

> *Dear Tori,*
> *I got myself in too deep and I'm not sure where to turn, so I'm sending this to you. I thought it would be easier to mail and have you look at it first, and then we can talk later. But no email. I'm concerned that someone could find out what I've been up to. I think someone has been following me.*

That's it? Come on, Sarah. At least you could have explained what this was about.

But then again, Sarah had probably been scared to say too much, and with good reason, given the danger she was in. Only it had gotten her killed anyway.

Tori detested the anger that surged through her. Anger at her sister for getting herself killed. She pushed down that hateful emotion—this wasn't Sarah's fault.

Goose bumps rose on her arms as she stuck the USB drive into the slot on her laptop.

She stared at incriminating documents about the company GenDynamics—the place where Sarah worked. And then it hit Tori. GenDynamics was an agricultural company. Of course! Now it was all beginning to make sense.

Tori should have looked into this from the beginning. She'd been too distraught to see clearly what was right there all the time.

Tori sat up and did a quick search on the company. GenDynamics produced pesticides and GMOs—genetically modified organisms. She'd heard the term repeatedly, but what exactly did that mean?

Tori read further. Gene splicing. That was what it was all about. DNA from a variety of species were forced into genes of other plants or animals. She cringed at what she read, and then went back to the information Sarah had gathered. Sarah had taken photographs of documentation that showed the company was purposefully mislabeling and selling an unapproved pesticide. If that was discovered, it could cost them tens of millions of dollars in fines, lawsuits and government penalties.

Comprehension slammed into her, and she flattened against the seat back.

Oh, Sarah...

She'd been part of an environmental group, and Tori had a feeling Dee knew about these other activities, but he'd been afraid to tell Tori. GenDynamics was a huge company with deep pockets. Maybe Sarah's run-in with the legislator was her way of trying to get someone to listen to her about what was going on there.

And when they wouldn't, she'd gathered this information herself.

Sarah had turned into a major whistle-blower. Whistle-blowers were supposed to be protected by laws, but they were often persecuted.

And in this case, she had been murdered before the whistle could be blown.

Tori's cell rang. Dad this time.

Tori grimaced. She couldn't talk to him at this moment. She had to process what all of this meant. Why hadn't Sarah given this information to Sanchez? She already had a working relationship with him. Instead, Sarah had sent the information to Tori so she could take action, and Tori had failed her sister.

Monumentally.

She couldn't go back in time to change any of it. All she could do was go forward and try to fix it now. She would find out who was behind Sarah's murder, thanks to this information she now had in her hands.

Tori's cell rang again. She would need to text Dad that she would call back in a bit. She opened the texting app to tell him and then stared at a text that had come through from Dad's cell.

If you want to see your parents alive bring me the package.

She replied with her own text. Wait. I'm at the airport. You'll have to give me time. I don't have it with me.

I know you have it with you.

Tori stared at her cell. Had he employed a listening app on her phone or on her parents'? Or was he watching her even now, here in the airport? Tori glanced around her. Goose bumps crawled over her.

If you want them to remain alive, you must tell no one. If the information in the package ever comes to light, their deaths will be on your hands. And then you'll die, too.

The street was dark and quiet when Ryan finally turned into his driveway and parked in the garage. He'd had to go back to the office to catch up on his reports and update his boss again, which meant he'd had to wait to find out what Katelyn wanted to show him. He found it was best to ferret out the truth before presenting anything to his boss.

Now he was ready to hear what she'd learned.

He hadn't asked her to stay and help, but he'd take any assistance he could get.

Ryan entered his home through the garage entrance and found the breakfast area dimly lit. Katelyn sat at the kitchen table, the light from her laptop reflecting on her face.

"Sorry I'm late. Captain Moran wanted a face-to-face with me." It had been good to be able to reassure his boss that Tori was no longer part of the investigation.

Now that Tori was at the airport, he realized just how glad he was that she was headed home. Maybe he would have caught the murderer by now, without her proximity and the fact she was in danger scrambling his brain.

And now he could focus on dousing what her presence had kindled inside of him.

And douse he would, though he wasn't sure how yet.

Starting tonight.

He grabbed sodas for each of them from the fridge, then pulled out the chair at the end of the table to sit. Ryan popped the top, drank and savored the fizz, then guzzled the rest. He sat the empty can on the table.

Katelyn finally responded.

"And you couldn't update him with this new information because you didn't have it, is that it?"

"Pretty much." He'd called her on the way to the office, but only got her voice mail. "So please enlighten me."

"You're still in love with her."

Her words struck him in the chest. "What?"

Katelyn finally pulled her attention from the laptop. "You heard me."

"Why are you saying this to me?"

Laughter burst from her. "So you admit it?"

"No. I admit nothing." He scraped a hand down his face. "That just came out of the blue." And it wasn't what he wanted to hear from his sister.

"Not out of the blue. You asked me to please enlighten you. So I did. I told you something you're ignoring."

He couldn't listen to this. Tori was gone and he had to get over her once and for all.

"I'm not in love with her," he said. "That ended a long time ago. How I feel has no bearing on finding Sarah's murderer and whoever is behind the attacks on Tori. She's going home now. Going back to work, where she'll be surrounded by FBI agents and be safe." He hoped. "Please explain your phone call to me. You said you found an interesting connection. Could you have been a little less cryptic? No, don't answer that. What have you learned?"

She rubbed her eyes. "I was looking into

Eddie Slattery when I came across a connection. I thought he could be connected to Sarah's place of employment, GenDynamics. He's not, but that's when I came across this interesting information."

Ryan stared at her laptop, at the two faces she'd pulled up.

"It could be nothing," she said.

"Or it could be everything."

SIXTEEN

Tori's palms slicked against the steering wheel. She'd taken a cab back to Sarah's to get her sister's car, and now she sat parked on the side of a dark road and looking at an empty building that had been condemned.

This monster had her parents in there?

Oh, Mom...

Anger raged in her veins. How dare he do this to her family? How dare he bring them into this?

Lord, please help me know how to play this. How do I get them back, safe and sound, and take this guy down?

If only she hadn't sent Ryan away, maybe he would be following her now as he had on multiple occasions, saving her from danger. She'd given him the cold shoulder in her need to get away from the situation, believing it was for the best.

But now her parents' lives were at stake.

Gripping her weapon, Tori quietly exited the car. She would likely be forced to give up the weapon, but she had another tucked away at her ankle.

Creeping forward, she held her weapon ready, prepared to use it if necessary. Wouldn't it be nice if she could surprise the kidnapper and killer and get the best of him...not that she thought it would ever be that easy.

She'd tucked the package in her purse. Maybe she shouldn't have brought it so she could have strung this guy out a little longer while she tried to save her parents.

At the building, she hesitated, mentally preparing herself to face whatever evil lurked inside with her parents.

Footfalls approached from behind. She stiffened.

"Don't move," a distorted voice said. "Toss the weapon and hold your hands up where I can see them."

Tori tossed her weapon, but not terribly far. "My parents?"

"In due time. Now, toss the other weapon, the one you keep at your ankle."

She heaved a sigh and removed the smaller pistol from the ankle strap, then shucked that, as well. Again, not too far. In a pinch, she might be able to reach it.

The distorted voice creeped her out. Then again, he was hiding his identity, which offered her hope that she and her parents might actually make it out of this alive. If he planned to kill them, there would be no reason to take such precautions to disguise himself.

"Keep walking and go inside the building."

Again Tori complied, her mind racing with how she could overtake this man. But she had to make sure her parents were alive and then get them someplace safe before she took action that could get them killed.

She stepped up to the doors.

"Open it."

"Look, there's no need to involve them."

"Open the door and go inside."

Tori did as she was told, stepping into a condemned and dark building, even though that went against every bit of instinct she had and all her training. But the threat to her parents trumped everything else.

A flashlight came on from behind, lighting her way ahead.

"Keep walking to the end of the hallway and then take a right."

Tori feared that her parents weren't here at all and she was only walking into a trap.

Lord, help me to get us out of this. Please save us.

In the long, dark hallway, she could see light up ahead of them, coming from beneath a doorway. A room in the middle of the building so no lights could be seen on the outside. No sniper shots to take out the person or people orchestrating the abduction.

She paused at the door from which light beamed. "This one?"

"Yes. Go inside and see your parents."

Tori opened the door and stepped inside. Her parents were both gagged and bound, sitting in chairs. Their eyes widened when they saw her. Short-lived relief rushed through her.

She started to move toward them to hug them.

"Stop."

Tori stopped, fear and anger surging through her. The terror in her parents' eyes nearly stole her breath. They both subtly shook their heads as if they wished she had stayed away. It shocked her that they expected her to save her own life and leave theirs to this monster.

"I assume the package is in your bag. Empty the contents on the floor."

She dumped everything out, suddenly wishing she'd done a more thorough search. What if Katelyn had planted another tracker and that was revealed now? She and her parents could die for that mistake. Who was she kidding—

they would die anyway. Even if the abductor hid his identity, they still knew too much. Sarah had known too much and had died for that.

Still, the thought of a tracker gave her hope. What if there really *had* been another tracker she hadn't found? That meant Ryan would know she had left the airport and wasn't on a plane to the far side of the country, if Katelyn still followed the tracker's data and shared that information with her brother.

"Kick the envelope away from you."

Tori kicked it away. The man morphing his voice stood behind her. She still hadn't seen his face. "All right. You have your package now. If you're thinking of killing us now, then you'd better think again."

He didn't respond.

"You told me if the information ever comes to light, then my parents' lives will be threatened again. The reverse is true—if something happens to them or to me—then I've made arrangements for everything to be revealed to the authorities. Do you understand?"

The words she was trying to use to gain their safe passage from this situation fell flat to her own ears.

"You're bluffing."

"I'm not. But if you kill us, you'll find out." Would he kill them and dump them in the river, or try to tie their murder to drugs like he'd tried with Sarah's death? He'd tried to make it look like she'd been in the wrong place at the wrong time and with the wrong group of people.

Whatever happened, she trusted Detective Ryan Bradley to discover the truth about their deaths.

Except Tori had no intention of letting it go that far.

She slowly began turning around.

"Stop!"

She continued turning, because if she wanted him to believe her about her threat, then she'd better start acting the part. Soon she faced off with a smallish figure dressed in black and wearing a mask.

Something looked strange about him.

He pulled off the mask.

Only he was a she. Blond hair spilled out over her shoulders.

"Who are you?"

That she'd revealed herself didn't bode well for them. Tori had pushed too far.

"You think you're so smart." The woman turned off the voice-distorting device. "I'd let you try to figure out who I am, except you're not leaving."

"What? That was our deal. And you know what's going to happen."

"It'll be too late by the time they figure it out, even if your threats are true."

Tori didn't get it. Why would it be too late? Unless… "You're leaving the country." Could Tori reach and disarm this woman in time?

"None of that is your concern any longer. Don't worry, I'm not going to kill you." The door opened and in stepped a muscular guy. "*He* is. Meet Vincent. It's easy to hire an assassin online these days. I'm glad he was around to finally get rid of Eddie, who botched everything, starting with those four murders."

The woman turned and then glanced back, tossing her hair over her shoulder. "Have fun, Vincent, but not too much fun. I want this all erased within the hour."

And she was gone.

Tori would have to face off with Vincent, but at least she had a chance to survive. A chance to save her parents. She wished she had called Ryan in, but it was too late for regrets now. Tori accepted the fact that Ryan wasn't coming. He wasn't following her.

She was on her own.

"It's just you and me now, big man. Drop the weapons and let's do this mano a mano." *Hand to hand.* "Or are you afraid to fight without your gun?"

His big arms still crossed, he grinned as if to say, "Challenge accepted."

This fight would test Tori in ways for which she hadn't prepared.

Her one advantage—this was a fight for her life and the lives of her parents.

Tori's kicks and punches didn't have the impact she'd hoped for. At least she was dodging the big man's attempts to harm her. Or was he simply toying with her?

With her efforts to hurt him, she slowly lured him away from her parents, hoping to give them a chance. A way out if they were able to take it.

She found herself situated between shelves filled with boxes of who knew what. Using her good shoulder, she rammed herself into the shelf. It toppled onto the beast.

A paint scraper slid across the floor. She grabbed it. She could cut her parents free.

Hurry. They had to hurry.

Catching her breath, Tori grabbed the scraper and started toward them.

A beefy hand closed around her ankle and squeezed. She cried out in pain as she fell to the floor. Twisting around, she tried to slice at him with the scraper, but she wasn't getting anywhere.

"Here!" She slid the scraper across the floor to her parents.

It stopped just short of her father's reach. Gripping her ankle, the mercenary pulled her closer while he slid from under the shelf.

In his eyes, she saw that he was done with the games.

Now he would kill her.

Ryan stepped into the fray as the big man was taking entirely too much pleasure in choking Tori, strangling her to death in front of her parents. With distance between them, he pointed the weapon at the man's head.

"Police! Release her now or I'll shoot!"

The man just held on tighter. Did he consider himself invincible? Ryan had called for backup, but he couldn't wait for them. Nor did he think he could wrestle this guy to the ground alone.

He fired his weapon, the sound exploding in his ears. The sight puncturing his heart as the man fell off Tori. Ryan removed his limp body completely and crouched next to her. Her hands around her throat, she sucked in air, then coughed. He gently assisted her into his lap and held her.

"Are you okay?" He was tired of asking that question and hoped this would be the last time for a good long while.

She nodded but couldn't speak.

Deputies and police officers streamed into the room and freed her parents. Ryan would have gotten to them, but concern for Tori filled all his thoughts.

She rested her hand against his shoulder. Relief surged inside. Relief and something he repeatedly tried to bury.

"How… How did you find me?" she croaked out. "Another tracker?"

"No. Please, don't talk. An ambulance should be here soon."

Her parents would have to be checked out, too. Right now they were giving their statements about their abduction, which gave him a few needed moments with Tori.

"Katelyn discovered that Suzanne Sanchez Tate, the owner of GenDynamics, where Sarah worked, was Agent Sanchez's sister. She married the man who started the company decades before and ran it with him until his death."

"That must be why Sarah sent the information to me instead of Agent Sanchez," Tori once again croaked out the words. "She was afraid she couldn't trust him with information on his sister. I wonder if he's guilty of playing a role in his sister's crimes or in covering up the real motive for the murders. But that still doesn't explain how you found me. Is there another tracker that I don't know about?"

"I think that your cell phone has been hacked and then tracked and that's how Mrs. Tate was able to follow you. She hired Eddie to kill you, but he failed. As for how I found you, I went to Mrs. Tate's home to question her. When I got there, she was driving away and I followed her instead—all the way here—and waited. Anyone who goes to an abandoned building in the middle of the night is up to no good."

Tori peered up at him, the admiration in her eyes overwhelming him.

"Thank you," she said. Her eyes widened. "But what about—"

"When I saw her forcing you down the hallway into this room, I called for backup quietly. I didn't want this to turn into a hostage situation—more than it already was. When she was on her way out, I cuffed her to a post in the building to hold her until I could check on you.

"Then I made my way to the room where she'd taken you. I missed the assassin going into the room. I'm just glad I got here in time." Ryan looked at Tori.

She appeared frazzled, with smudges on her face. Wild hair. Bright eyes.

He loved her so much.

God, will I ever get a chance with her?

He knew the answer to that. No. No, he wouldn't.

Finally the paramedics arrived and took Tori from Ryan, not for the first time. He didn't want to let her go, but she'd sustained more injuries. Once again she was taken to the hospital. At least she was safe and had survived— her parents, too.

At least this was over.

And that would mean his time with her was over, too.

Ryan turned his focus to policing matters. Deputies placed Suzanne Tate in the back of a vehicle to cart off to a holding cell on murder charges, as well as kidnapping. There could be more charges as they dug deeper into the activities she'd killed to hide.

Three days later, Ryan sat at his desk filling out reports and completing paperwork. He'd killed a man to save Tori, and that required an investigation into the incident regardless of the circumstances. Given the nature of additional financial and environmental crimes committed by Mrs. Tate, the feds were also involved in peeling back the layers. Agent Sanchez's activities were under scrutiny, as well.

It was hard to accept that Sarah's attempt at

whistle-blowing to expose harmful behavior had ultimately ended in her death and that of her friends. Harder still to deal with the fact that she'd reached out for Tori's help. The guilt that she hadn't been there for her sister when her assistance could possibly have saved her continued to distress Tori. Moving beyond that would take time, if she ever got over it.

Just like it would take Ryan time to get over her.

Although trusting Tori with his heart was a huge risk, deep down, he'd always known it was a risk he would take again if given the chance. When her life had been in danger he'd realized just how much he wanted a second chance with her.

But that wasn't going to happen, and Ryan would have to be okay with it. He would survive, just like he had before.

Tori was alive and well, and he wished her the best.

A ruckus drew his attention from his computer. Katelyn smiled as she approached.

He pushed back from the desk. "What are you doing here?"

"I have a surprise for you. Can you come with me?"

He blew out a breath. "You aren't trying to

fix me up with someone, are you? I'm really not in the mood."

"No. Nothing as nefarious as that." Katelyn led him through the sheriff's department offices and out the door, then around the corner to the small coffee shop.

Sitting at a table in the back corner, Tori smiled at him.

His heart almost stopped and he stumbled forward. "What's going on, Katelyn?"

He'd told himself he would be okay going forward without her, but he couldn't take more torture.

"Come on." Katelyn pulled him forward.

Tori stood from the table. "Hi, Ryan. It's good to see you."

She wore a flattering scarf around her neck, presumably to hide the bruises that likely remained.

"You, too." He slowly sat at the table with his sister and Tori. "So what's this about?"

I thought you'd gone home.

Katelyn appeared giddy as a schoolgirl and her laugh almost sounded like a giggle. "Well, Tori and I have an announcement."

"The suspense is killing me. Really. What's going on?"

Tori pressed a hand on Katelyn's arm. "We're starting up our own private and protective services business. We need to come up with a snazzy name."

His heart jumped around inside. "Wow. Well, that was fast. Are you sure?"

"Yes," Katelyn said. "Absolutely."

He wanted to hear Tori's take on this. Had Katelyn pressured her? Not that it was easy to make Tori do anything.

"So will this business be something you do from across the country?" he dared to ask her.

"I'm moving back, Ryan," she said. "I've already handed in my resignation."

Hope surged. Hope and caution.

"Well that's my cue to give you some privacy." Smiling, Katelyn slipped from her chair. "I'll be over there, eyeing the ice-cream cones."

Ryan breathed in slowly. Braced himself for what she would say.

"Can we take a walk?" Tori asked. "It's a beautiful day."

"Sure." He fought the need to run from this torture. Run far away from what he knew she could do to his heart.

Outside, they walked over to a small park with a stream. He waited patiently for her to speak her piece. Finally they stopped, next to a thick-trunked pine. In the distance, he could see Mount Shasta, magnificent and beautiful.

But the mountain's beauty was nothing compared to Tori's. She was doing it to him again. Warmth spilled out of his heart through his chest. He wanted to let himself love her.

Katelyn had been right—he was still in love with Tori. He wanted the freedom to give in to that.

"Mom and Dad urged me to go back to my job and my life. Funny, I thought working with the FBI was what I wanted." Tori stared at the small, trickling brook for two breaths, then lifted her gaze to him. "But the job I thought I loved, the life I thought I wanted, that's all changed."

"What are you saying, exactly?"

"I don't have the right to ask, Ryan, after everything I've put you through, but I hope you'll give me another chance. Give *us* another chance. Because I would choose you, choose this life here, over anything else in the world. I know that now. I'm so sorry I didn't see that before. But if you don't want that chance with me, I'll walk away. I'll understand."

In an instant, his lips were pressed against hers. His arms were around her, and she responded with tenderness, and something more just under the surface. He eased away enough to whisper, "I love you. I've always loved you."

"I love you, too, Ryan. Forgive me."

"There's nothing to forgive." Just… Ryan

eased away but held her closely. "I don't want to lose you again. Lose you to your job or—"

"You won't, I promise."

"Then why don't we make it official?" His palms slicked. He could be pushing her too fast. She might not be ready for this. "Will you marry me?"

"Are you sure about this?"

"I've never been more sure of anything." His heart pounded. What would she say?

She lifted her chin and kissed him. Thoroughly. Then she said, "Does that answer your question?"

His head dizzy, he peered at her green eyes. "I think that's a yes, but I'd love to hear that on your lips."

Your beautiful lips.

"Yes, Ryan Bradley. Yes, I'll marry you."

* * * * *

Look for more books in Elizabeth Goddard's Mount Shasta Secrets miniseries, coming in 2020!

Dear Reader,

Thank you so much for reading *Deadly Evidence*! I hope you enjoyed the story and the first book in my newest series, Mount Shasta Secrets. As you might have figured out by now if you've read my other books, I love beautiful settings that usually include mountains or a Pacific Northwest coastline.

In *Deadly Evidence*, tragedy struck Tori's life when her sister was murdered. Through that tragedy, Tori's perspectives changed drastically. Unfortunately, that's exactly what it sometimes takes to make us realize what's truly important in life—the friends and family around us whom we should appreciate and not take for granted. Whom we should take the time to cherish and love.

But it doesn't have to take a tragedy for us to savor the time we have with our loved ones and prioritize what is truly important. I hope and pray you treasure those around you while you can.

I love hearing from my readers. You can find out ways to contact me—Facebook, Twitter, Instagram, etc.—through my website at elizabethgoddard.com.

Many blessings!
Elizabeth Goddard

Get 4 FREE REWARDS!

We'll send you 2 FREE Books plus <u>plus</u> 2 FREE Mystery Gifts.

Love Inspired® books feature contemporary inspirational romances with Christian characters facing the challenges of life and love.

FREE
Value Over
$20

Get 4 FREE REWARDS!

We'll send you 2 FREE Books plus 2 FREE Mystery Gifts.

Harlequin® Heartwarming™ Larger-Print books feature traditional values of home, family, community and—most of all—love.

FREE Value Over **$20**

THE FORTUNES OF TEXAS COLLECTION!

18 FREE BOOKS in all!

Treat yourself to the rich legacy of the Fortune and Mendoza clans in this remarkable 50-book collection. This collection is packed with cowboys, tycoons and Texas-sized romances!

YES! Please send me **The Fortunes of Texas Collection** in Larger Print. This collection begins with 3 FREE books and 2 FREE gifts in the first shipment. Along with my 3 free books, I'll also get the next 4 books from The Fortunes of Texas Collection, in LARGER PRINT, which I may either return and owe nothing, or keep for the low price of $5.24 U.S./$5.89 CDN each plus $2.99 for shipping and handling per shipment*. If I decide to continue, about once a month for 8 months I will get 6 or 7 more books but will only need to pay for 4. That means 2 or 3 books in every shipment will be FREE! If I decide to keep the entire collection, I'll have paid for only 32 books because 18 books are FREE! I understand that accepting the 3 free books and gifts places me under no obligation to buy anything. I can always return a shipment and cancel at any time. My free books and gifts are mine to keep no matter what I decide.

☐ 269 HCN 4622   ☐ 469 HCN 4622

Name (please print)

Address   Apt. #

City   State/Province   Zip/Postal Code

Mail to the **Reader Service:**
IN U.S.A.: P.O Box 1341, Buffalo, N.Y. 14240-8531
IN CANADA: P.O. Box 603, Fort Erie, Ontario L2A 5X3

COMING NEXT MONTH FROM
Love Inspired® Suspense

Available October 1, 2019

COURAGE UNDER FIRE
True Blue K-9 Unit • by Sharon Dunn

Rookie K-9 officer Lani Branson's one goal in her training exercise is to prove herself capable of the job—until she's attacked. Now a ruthless stalker's threatening her at every turn, and her boss, Chief Noah Jameson, and his K-9 partner have made it their mission to keep her alive.

HIDDEN IN AMISH COUNTRY
Amish Country Justice • by Dana R. Lynn

There's a bull's-eye on her back, and Sadie Standings can't remember why... yet she trusts Amish widower Ben Mast to protect her. But when hiding the *Englischer* endangers the single dad and his young son, Ben and Sadie must rely on each other and her murky memory to catch a murderer.

CHRISTMAS WITNESS PROTECTION
Protected Identities • by Maggie K. Black

When Corporal Holly Asher's witness protection transportation is targeted, going on the run with Detective Noah Wilder is the only way to survive. But can they pose as an engaged couple at Christmas without tipping off those who want to kill her?

COVERT CHRISTMAS TWIN
Twins Separated at Birth • by Heather Woodhaven

After discovering she's a twin, FBI special agent Kendra Parker tracks down her birth mother—and faces a barrage of bullets. Now armed with the knowledge that her mother's a spy, Kendra must work with FBI analyst Joe Rose to find the government mole threatening her family...before they all end up dead.

KILLER AMNESIA
by Sherri Shackelford

Emma Lyons's investigative reporting skills are put to the test when she loses her memory after an attempt on her life. But researching her own past with the help of Deputy Liam McCourt leads to town secrets darker than they imagined...and a killer who won't stop until they're silenced.

ALASKAN CHRISTMAS COLD CASE
by Sarah Varland

For years, a serial killer has eluded authorities—and now Alaska state trooper Erynn Cooper is in his sights. With help from small-town police chief Noah Dawson, can she finally stop the murders before Christmas...or will Erynn become the next victim?

LOOK FOR THESE AND OTHER LOVE INSPIRED BOOKS WHEREVER BOOKS ARE SOLD, INCLUDING MOST BOOKSTORES, SUPERMARKETS, DISCOUNT STORES AND DRUGSTORES.

LISCNM0919